Earthrunner
and the War of Water

Simone Pakavakis
Constantine Pakavakis

Glass House Books
Brisbane

Acknowledgements

Cover design: Shannon Boland

Book design: David P Reiter

Writing our first novel has been an experience graced with the goodwill, kindness and expertise of so many people who have supported our writing in some way. In particular, we wish to thank IP's Dr David Reiter and his editors Emma-Clare Daly and James Devitt for their guidance and patience throughout the publishing process; Shannon Boland for her creative illustration and design on our cover; Irina Dunn, our literary agent, for imparting on us our first editing tips and championing our manuscript; Kelly Gardiner for providing insights through a manuscript assessment; Maureen McCarthy for her series of writing workshops in our early stages; Amelia Donnelly, for her encouragement and note sharing; George Lianos and Elise Zouck for use of their homely writing haven; Grant Allen for sharing his beekeeping experience; our wonderful supportive family and friends, especially Caitlin, Janine and Alec; and finally, our spoodle Alby, for teaching us all about the affection of a dog.

Glass House Books

Earthrunner and the War of Water

Simone and Constantine Pakavakis are the daughter and father co-authors of *Earthrunner*.

Growing up with her head in the books of esteemed Australian authors like John Marsden and Markus Zusak, Simone was a runner-up in several writing competitions before winning the Slade Literary Award in Year 10 for her short story, 'The Big Game.' The story became a short film, featuring in the Melbourne International Film Festival (2014).

In addition to her love for writing, Simone has a passion for the integral development of children. After graduating from the University of Melbourne, Simone began teaching at an inner-city primary school. She works to promote kindness as a core strength in her students and sees literacy skills and quality children's literature as key elements for this.

Constantine has published a non-fiction work, *Looking Inside*, and was co-author of *Early Moves – Primary Gender Inclusive Curriculum Units*, a text for teachers.

He has been a primary school teacher since 1988 and has also worked as an education officer at Scienceworks, where he led the creation of the Nitty Gritty Super City exhibition. A video he produced with his class about climate change, *Solar Solution*, won the 1999 Ford "One Planet" Environment Award.

Prior to teaching, Constantine worked briefly in Civil Engineering, was a draft resistor during the Vietnam War, became a meditation and yoga teacher in India, and taught Tantra Yoga for ten years in Italy, Greece, India and Australia.

Constantine continues to advocate for human rights, social justice and peace and climate action as an active member and supporter of various activist organisations.

Glass House Books
Brisbane

Glass House Books
an imprint of IP (Interactive Publications Pty Ltd)
Treetop Studio • 9 Kuhler Court
Carindale, Queensland, Australia 4152
sales@ipoz.biz
http://ipoz.biz

Printed in 12 pt Adobe Caslon Pro on 14 pt Avenir Book.

ISBN: 978192830135 (PB); 978192830142 (eBk)

A catalogue record for this book is available from the National Library of Australia

Authors' Note

In February 2003, more than one hundred thousand people gathered in Melbourne, Australia and marched for peace to protest against Australia's involvement in an impending war against Iraq. Amongst them was our family: Simone (8), Caitlin (6), Janine and Constantine. Returning home on the tram, Simone had many questions: Why did there need to be a war? What were the other options?

A family discussion ensued around a historical story from 'Buddhism' by Christmas Humphries, which involves a war over water being averted. Simone related an incident from school camp, where she and a friend protected some ducklings by standing in front of them, shielding the animals from classmates throwing stones. The similarities between the ancient incident and that of the children was striking.

As a result of these conversations and a mutual love for writing, the partnership for *Earthrunner* was born, and Simone and Constantine began the backbone of a story that used these ideas as a core. As Simone grew, so did the story, particularly during school holidays and family vacations. The draft manuscript accepted for publication by Interactive Publications was completed while Simone began her work as a primary school teacher.

Dedicated to every person, young and old, who has taken a step for peace.

In a gentle way, you can shake the world.
– *Gandhi*

Contents

Historical Setting of *Earthrunner*

The fictional story of *Earthrunner* is set in the kingdom of Gandhara in the North West of ancient India, now Pakistan. It is the year 330 BCE, three years before the arrival of Alexander the Great (mentioned in *Earthrunner* as 'Ksanda'), who sought to conquer the known world.

Historians mention animosity between Ambhika, Prince of Gandhara, and Purushattama, King of the neighbouring Paurava, but little is written about the nature of their conflict. The preparation for a war over water between these two monarchs in *Earthrunner* is invented as an explanation of the animosity. How likely would this have been? These were rich agriculturally based kingdoms and in times of drought, water was critical. Geological records indicate that climate change was a significant factor in the collapse of the Indus Valley Civilization that had previously flourished in the area. This civilization went into decline largely due to the drying up of a water system to the east of the Indus, leaving a sub-Indus culture behind.

Further Historical Notes are at the end of the book.

Chapter 1: India, 330 BCE

Leeta

"**S**top!" I called, as if they were going to listen. They didn't. I started after them. Closer, closing, I ran into their dust. In a single motion, they swooped up stones and threw.

"Don't!" I cried, too late.

Their stones pounded the earth, frightening the monkeys that had almost reached the nearest mango tree.

"Patish!" I said, reaching his side as he came to a halt.

He ignored me, his twin sister, and turned to face Satu, his best friend. Wide grins spread across their faces.

Arriving behind me, Asten, Tomay, Liddu and Sujas broke into a victory chant. "Pa-tish! Sa-tu!"

"Did you see those monkeys scatter?" cried Tomay. "Pa-tish! Sa-tu!"

Patish and Satu glowed, heroes of the moment.

"Where are the monkeys?" said Seera, our younger sister, arriving at the scene. "I want to see them too!" She balanced on the tips of her toes trying to look over the tall grasses.

"They got away," I answered, loud enough for the boys to hear. They didn't seem to care. "Come, Seera, let's go."

I beckoned her towards the Well. She held out her hand.

In our village, Shaktin, the Well was a place of worship. Its water gave us life, and just being near water felt cool in this heat. Every afternoon, half the village came out here and stood around the Well chatting, waiting their turn for water. Even the stray dogs that survived on our scraps loved lying in the dirt around the Well, waiting for a drink. People would wash themselves on the stone slabs surrounding it, though no one dared to at the moment. The rains were so late, and the water was so low. What if it ran out? What would we do then?

The words of Tanu the trader had haunted me since his visit a few days ago.

"Water is life," he'd said, giving his camels a generous drink. "That's why Prince Ambhika will never let Taxila end up like Harappa, ruined when their water dried up. You've all heard the rumours, haven't you? War. The King of Paurava is threatening a war over the water of the river Jhelum."

The mere mention of war made me shudder. War was what killed Father. Since Tanu's warning, I couldn't decide which was the most terrifying: the possibility of another war, or our kingdom dying from thirst.

I took Seera's outstretched hand and started to walk when the buzzing of the evening cicadas stopped. They were silent, all of them, not only the ones near us. It was eerie.

"What is it?" I murmured.

Then they started again, but their hum was different. Was something troubling them? No one else seemed to notice except for one of the strays – the skinny one with a missing front leg. Limpy. He raised his head, tilting it to one side. His ears stood tall, listening.

"Alright," I said to the boys. "You've frightened those monkeys away, so let's get back to the Well, or there'll be no water to cook with."

"You go, Leeta," said Liddu. "You mind our place in the queue. We need to stay. The monkeys are after our mangoes."

Asten, Tomay and Sujas all nodded their agreement. Patish awkwardly said nothing. I turned my eyes to the ground. I didn't mean to sound like Mother.

"But what about the bananas?" added Sujas, wanting to go on with the argument. "There's some of them ripening too."

Satu stepped in. "They're gone, but we'll be ready for them tomorrow," he said, turning to walk back.

He always came to Patish's aid. I watched them as they glanced at each other.

"Good. Come, Seera, let's go…" I looked down, expecting her to be there. She wasn't.

"Over there – a monkey!" Seera's eyes shone. She loved finding things that were hidden to others. It was almost as if they called out to her in words only she could hear.

I edged over to the clearing. Seera was right – there lay the shape of a monkey. It was still. The boys, just within earshot, sprung back and scattered to pick up stones.

"We must have hit it!" cried Liddu, acting as if he had been right to want to stay. "Let's finish it off just in case..."

Seera and I joined hands and raced to block their target.

"Don't hurt it anymore!" I said.

"Get out of the way!" Tomay demanded.

"Move, Leeta!" added Liddu.

I looked to Patish, but he stood motionless. His loyalty to his fellow hunters was confusing. Where was the brother I knew? Our platted Rakhi bracelets were around his wrist, the ones Seera and I had tied at the last Festival of Colours in exchange for his blessings and pledge of protection for life. I touched my own hemp string bracelet and felt the tiny dangling Earthmother figurine he had carved from sandalwood. Seera saw me and copied, fingering the bracelet and the figurine on her right wrist.

Patish watched. He knew us well enough to guess what we were thinking, but it made no difference. How easily his loyalty to his sisters was forgotten when his friends were around! Seera and I said nothing. We didn't have to.

Even though such raids by monkeys were common, Patish and his friends had never killed one before. But they were older, now. Most of them had seen fourteen summers, except for Liddu, the youngest, who was only twelve. Their arms were stronger and their aims better.

Tomay stepped forward. "You heard us, Leeta, move! Who do you think you are, anyway? Some Earthmother goddess, protector of all wild animals or something?"

I eyed Patish. Would he protect me from this insult?

I decided not to wait. "Your mocking words have no power, Tomay. The Earth is my mother as she is yours. I can stand wherever I want, just as you can."

As Patish opened his mouth, a distant rumbling echoed from the valley, and we turned towards it. Limpy stopped and growled, his tail down between his legs. With darkness setting in, we couldn't see much.

"Distant thunder?" Tomay guessed.

"No clouds," Satu said. "Sounds more like an earthquake!"

"But the earth's not shaking," said Sujas.

Patish gazed intently, his forehead wrinkling as if that might help him see. "Let's get going," he said.

No one argued, and handfuls of stones hit the earth as the boys started walking back.

Ignoring them, Seera and I darted toward the monkey.

"What are you doing?" Patish called out. "Come on!" There was a seriousness in his voice, the sound of responsibility he used whenever Mother was involved. He might let his sisters down, but never Mother.

"We're coming, but we can't just leave the monkey to die," I called back, hoping it wasn't already dead.

"It could bite," said Seera, looking to me for reassurance.

"Those boys!" I said, bending down. "Poor little thing."

"Leeta... I believe in you," she said in her cute little-sister-way. "You may not be an Earthmother, but you caught up with them before. You are an Earthrunner!"

In the fading light, I could barely make out a bloody gash on the monkey's head, just above its left eye. I tore a narrow strip of cloth from the bottom of my dress and carefully lifted its head to wrap the wound.

"Is it still alive?" asked Seera. "Can we take it home?"

"Can't you hear that rumbling?" Patish said, arriving. "Hurry up! Mother will be worrying, and here you are talking about bringing a dead monkey home, as if we'd eat it!"

He was joking, but I could see the worried look on his face. He looked back at his friends who had already reached the huts. They were barely visible from the smoke of dung patties smouldering inside fireplaces.

"Come on, Seera," he said, half pleading, half ordering, as he held out his hand.

Seera held both her arms up. "Uppa?"

Patish gave her a silent nod. She smiled, climbed up onto a log, and jumped onto his back. This was the Patish I knew, the one I'd always known.

4

I shook my head. "You always give in... she'll always be your little baby," I teased, remembering the comment Mother had made when I complained about it once: "That's love."

"Quickly," Patish insisted, "Let's go."

As he spoke, the monkey opened its eyes. It looked right at me then scampered off, its white headband visible until it disappeared amongst the grasses.

"You saved it – happy now?" said Patish. "Come on!"

We hastened back towards the Well. The last of the boys had left carrying pots of water on their shoulders.

Patish put Seera down and lowered the pail into the water. "Never seen it so low," he said. "Go on, walk ahead." He filled the water pot he'd left there earlier, hauled it up onto his shoulder and quickly caught up to us.

It was then that I felt the earth pounding beneath my feet. For a moment, I thought it was his footsteps, heavy with the weight of the water, so I swung around to help him. Patish was staring at something.

"Run, Leeta!" he yelled. "Seera, run, RUN!"

Chapter 2: Taken for War

Patish

R iders – it could be a raid! The rumours of war...
      Leeta and Seera ran towards Mother, whose silhouette stood outside our hut. There was no time to think, the riders were heading for me. I braced, ready to fight, the pot of water my only weapon.

Red - I stopped. It was the uniform of our own army!

Three defenders of Gandhara dismounted in front of me.

"Welcome to Shaktin," I said, unsure of what was happening. Mother hurried towards us and burst past the soldiers.

"Patish!" she cried, hugging me.

"Mother, they're from..." I began.

"I am his Mother," she said, taking control. "What do you want with him?"

Leeta and Seera arrived just behind her, perplexed.

"Respected Mother," began the soldier, "your son is needed for..."

"What?" Mother cried. "It cannot be! I am a widow, and my children are all that I have!"

The soldier's eyes flicked over at me.

"By the Royal Word, all males of sturdy body are summoned for the Army of Gandhara. That's any boy taller than this."

As he spoke, his muscular arm tapped a staff on the ground. It was a stern length of bamboo, cut cleanly at the end. The top reached to my eyes. I stared, realising what it meant.

"NO!" Mother bellowed. "He's just a boy! You're conscripting *boys*!"

The soldier's expression didn't change.

Mother tried to compose herself by pressing her hands together in front of her chest as if in prayer. "I beg you," she said, "Patish is only fourteen. My husband was killed in the last war, and Patish is my only son!"

The soldier dropped his gaze. "My orders are to conscript every male taller than this staff."

He straightened up and looked at the younger soldiers holding the reins of the horses. They said nothing. No sympathy from these hardened soldiers.

I never thought soldiers would do something like this. We'd often played soldiers, but we always played them as heroes… risking our lives to protect our families, saving our country from evil invaders. We idolised them, and, even though I had lost Father in a war, I dreamt of being a soldier, of becoming a hero like he had been.

I could see the distress on Mother's face.

"Your orders must be wrong," she said. "Patish hasn't even had the sacred Ritual of Manhood. Everyone knows you can only conscript men who have had the sacred ritual!"

"A special ritual will be held for the new conscripts," the soldier answered.

Mother looked into his eyes. She had a way of seeing through to the real person.

"Please," she said, soul to soul, "I beg you! Please don't take my child."

The soldier paused, perhaps he was a father himself. I hoped he understood us.

"Orders are orders," he said. "The Word of the Prince must be followed."

Mother just stood there, wounded.

"You have time to gather a few things for your son before we march," the soldier continued. "Make haste. We are assembling the conscripts near the Well."

Leeta moved toward Seera. Her lip had dropped and her eyes glazed. "Quick," she said, "we must pack what we can for Patish before they leave."

She took Seera in one hand, Mother in the other, and led them off.

***

The able-bodied men and tall-enough boys were being organised into two lines. Mothers, wives, daughters, sisters, and a few young boys and old men looked on, helpless. Finally, I saw Mother, Leeta and Seera arriving.

Mother rushed over and embraced me. Tears rolled down her cheeks.

A flood of tears ran down my face. "Mother…" I started, wanting to console her, but I didn't know how.

She held my face between her hands and kissed the top of my head. She spoke softly, "Patish, my son, don't try to be a hero… just come back alive. There is no greater heroism than living and working for your family. These wars are the games of kings, and there is no honour in killing, so do anything you have to, to survive. Promise me this, Patish."

I loved Mother more than life itself. Now I had to leave her to fight in a war. It didn't make sense. I hated no one; I had no enemies. I glanced at the soldier then back into Mother's eyes.

"I promise, Mother." I said, my hand clutching Father's sun disk around my neck, extracting from it every bit of power it had to make my oath come true. "By my Father's Sun, I swear I will come back to you, Seera and Leeta."

Being killed was a thought I couldn't allow, but it wouldn't go away. I felt it circling like a vulture from a distance, watching, waiting. Leaving my family without a man to look after them was intolerable.

Mother held my cheeks in her hands. "I call on the Great Father Sun to protect you with every ray of light and may every power of the Earthmother help to bring you home safe!" She kissed my forehead, adding: "And may your inner eye guide your every step."

Seera stepped forward, raising her arms, and beckoning with a frown.

"Uppa!"

I lifted her up for our special hug. Her warm breath in my ear melted my heart. I put Seera down and faced Leeta with blurry eyes. For the first time, we were being separated.

"Leeta, I'm sorry… sometimes… you know, with my friends…"

"Prepare to leave," came a command.

8

"My brother," said Leeta. "I knew you would never neglect us. Now take this pack, just a few of your things."

"That's enough," ordered the Commander. "Soldiers, straighten your lines. Make your village proud!"

Proud, I thought, Shaktin is prouder of us than you could ever imagine!

Trembling, Mother, Leeta and Seera moved back, joining the rest of our villagers. We all knew what could happen in war.

I stood near Liddu – a hint of a smile betrayed his excitement. He stood with his older brother Rakul, a tall, stringy young man who had only recently married, and their stern, grey-haired father, Martal, a powerful man who had fought in the last war. It was Martal who had taken Mother and other widows back to the battlefield where their slain husbands lay. Diipundi had gone with them to guide the rituals of fire that helped the souls of the dead enter the mysterious realms of the afterworld. Mother was always grateful to Martal for taking her, heavily pregnant as she was, even though they had arrived too late to find Father's body. Many of the dead had already been cremated in huge collective pyres. Mother told us how she had still performed the death rites, farewelling ashes from the pyre near where Father had died.

"Soldiers!" the Commander called. "Ready, forward!"

We were to be the soldiers. We began to walk. The air thickened with dust from so many feet and hooves stirring the dry earth of the village path.

I imagined how Mother was feeling. The last time she had seen Father alive was when he looked back at her as he marched off after being conscripted. Just like this. I'd held her hand as we waved Father goodbye. She was so pregnant with Seera that she couldn't run after me when I broke away from her to run after him.

And then there was the day the survivors returned. How Mother gasped when she couldn't see Father amongst them.

"He died a hero in the service of his king," a survivor had said, handing her back the necklace they had recovered from his body.

That was the strangest, saddest day of my life. Until today.

Chapter 3: Sisters in Womanhood

Leeta

Their words echoed inside my head: "Orders are orders..."
The "Royal Word," they'd said.
The "Word of the Prince," they'd said.
Then they took Patish for their war.

They were out of sight now, having disappeared into the night. Above us, the stars were cheerless without the moon. The whole village stood under that sky, speechless, gazing into the dark.

Without thinking, we started drifting back towards the place we went when we needed each other most, our communal hut, The Circle.

I loved spending evenings here, singing and chanting stories about our ancestors that drifted into the fields and skies above. Earthmother must also have enjoyed the love and devotion we showed Her. And it's here where we held our Rituals of Womanhood and Manhood after the first rains of the season.

A small oil lamp sat in the centre of the floor space, its flickering flame throwing light around the room. Diipundi was there, too, his eyes closed in meditation. Diipundi was revered in our village. There wasn't a family he hadn't helped through times of illness with his potions and herbs; not a person he hadn't guided or consoled with his wisdom and his memorised verses from the sages of the past. He was a grandfather to us, especially the little children who would reel with laughter at his stories and magical tricks.

Everyone entered silently and sat in a circle around the light. Seera and I sat on either side of Mother. Like the motionless Diipundi and everyone else, we closed our eyes, allowing the aroma of sandalwood to soothe our troubled thoughts. The humming of cicadas and the croaking of frogs filled the silence as we waited respectfully for him to speak.

Diipundi's eyes opened gently and then so did everyone else's. He looked around, making eye contact with each of us. "In your eyes, I see terror. The rumours of a war with Paurava have been confirmed and our worst fears have come to life. Once again, our men have been taken to fight and the long wait begins with our prayers for their safe return."

"Respected Diipundi," a voice interrupted, "why have they taken my twelve-year-old Liddu?" It was Jasmin and in her voice was the pain of all the mothers.

"So, it is not only Rakul and Martal from your family, Mother Jasmin, but young Liddu as well." Diipundi paused for a moment, nodding. Then he turned to us. "And from your eyes, Mother Lallina Devi, I see they have taken Patish."

Many voices cried out, but Mother was heard above the others. "Diipundiji," she thundered. "Respected Elder and Carer of our village, I am here not for solace, but to beg you to show us a way to save our children from this war. Like Liddu, my Patish has not even had his Manhood Ritual. Since when has this been our Way? We are not warriors. It is not right to take the young. Is it even right to fight such a war? We all know the horrors and the pain and suffering it will bring."

"Lallina Devi, my son and my husband have been conscripted too," said Kamilla, mother of Asten, "but I cannot agree with your words. To oppose the prince would bring ruin to us all. Besides, we aren't even sure the war will happen. The King of Paurava may back down. He surely must know that, in a war with Gandhara, there would be no victor, only devastation on both sides."

"That may be right," argued Tadesh, one of the few old men left in the village, "but if we don't stop the Pauravans' demands on our water now, we will all be worse off in times of drought. If the royal fields don't get enough water, they'll increase the taxes from villages like ours!"

"You talk of water, but I talk of the life of my son, and of your sons and husbands," Mother replied. "How can I just sit and wait in the hope that my child will be returned alive?

"This war is not right." she continued. "The Pauravans have been our friends ever since I can remember. Some of us even have Pauravan ancestors and living relatives. There's always been enough water for all of us, so why do we have to go to war over it now?"

No one else spoke. All eyes turned to Diipundi.

"Let us weigh up the situation carefully," he said. "As the Purple Sage has said, 'When confronted by a dangerous rhino, stand still so it cannot distinguish you from a tree.' Kamilla is correct to point out the perils of opposing the prince. We do not want to increase the peril we already face, and to act brashly could ruin the chances of those we would wish to save.

"Kamilla has also raised the question of the strength of the Pauravans. It has taken us all by shock that the prince's decree has included even fourteen-year-olds. Why would this be necessary? Perhaps there is more to this than we know."

Diipundi shook his head. "My dear Tadesh, you fought side by side with Pauravans to repel the invading hordes many years ago. Lallina Devi values the peace we have with our neighbours; and she has good reason to question the need for such a war as we face now. We must consider her words, but we must not rush. Go home now to rest and let us ponder these things in the stillness of the night."

The villagers rose and began to leave, talking amongst themselves.

When most were gone, Mother stood up, took a few steps and knelt down in front of Diipundi. "My mind hears the wisdom of your words, oh Carer of our village, but my heart cannot stand still. It yearns to act... our loved ones are in danger!"

Seera and I sat just behind her. Diipundi smiled at us before answering.

"Your heart is true, Mother Lallina Devi, but what then would you do?"

"I don't know, but I do know I must do something!"

I finally found the courage to speak. "Respected Diipundi, you've told us lots of stories about the Purple Sage... what would the Wise One do?"

"Only the Wise One can answer that," he said, nodding to me.

"Well, then... can we... let's ask the Wise One!"

Mother stared at me, then turned to Diipundi. "Diipundi, you have spoken often of the wisdom of the Compassionate One, let us seek out this wisdom now!"

Diipundi paused, his eyes still. Every wrinkle of his forehead gathered in a frown. "My child, I am too old and weak for such a journey. Even if I could, it would take too long, and it would be too late! Besides, it is years since I have heard any news of the Purple Sage. Even the illumination of wisdom does not bring immortality. The Wise One may well have passed on from this world to the next."

"But if you don't know this for certain, the Wise One may still be alive!" Mother said.

Diipundi was silent.

I sat up straight, and, before he could respond, I blurted out, "I'll go! I'm the fastest runner in the village now." I hadn't meant to be so boastful, but it was true, since the boys had been conscripted.

Mother frowned, then reached out to touch my cheek. "How could I risk your safety, Leeta?"

"Mother, I can do it – I know I can," I insisted. "I'm not afraid!"

Diipundi examined my resolve. "Leeta is an exceptionally brave and resourceful girl," he said gently. "Perhaps it is right to give her the chance to save her twin brother, regardless of how slender that chance may be."

The flame of the burning wick seemed brighter as I waited for her reply.

"Lallina Devi," Diipundi said, "this is not an easy decision to make. I can see that your mind is split in two. Do you risk your daughter to save your son, or do you accept things as they are and let fate run its course?"

Diipundi then turned to me. "Leeta, your courage has always been obvious, and you have wisdom beyond your years. Why, you could be a Wise One yourself!" He turned to Seera and added: "And little Seera, why you're the little Purple Sage of our village. Between the three of you, you have the wisdom to make the right decision. But now I suggest you all go home and sleep. Lallina Devi, let it settle for a while and make the decision in the freshness of the morning. The coolness of the night will help your mind to set."

Mother held our hands.

"Please, Mother, we must try," I said.

She spoke to Diipundi once more. "My mind is made up. I can't believe I'm saying this, but there is no choice, the fire of injustice burns too strongly inside me. I cannot accept my boy having to fight in such a war. Now my only question is should I go with Leeta, or should all three of us go?"

Another voice emerged from the darkness. "Such a dangerous journey needs more than one. But Lallina Devi, you and Seera would only slow Leeta down. My Anula could keep up with her. The only way this could have a real chance of success is if Anula and Leeta go together."

Through the dim light, I made out the shape of Hileena, mother of Anula, a glimmer in her piercing eyes.

Of all the girls in the village, it was Anula who I really didn't get along with. If there was such a thing as opposites, we were it. Both our fathers had been killed in the same war, but after the war her family left Shaktin to live with her mother's sister who was a palace maid. But they returned to the village to support Hileena's aging mother, and Anula had been trying to establish herself as the leader of the village girls ever since.

I looked into the darkness, but I couldn't see Anula anywhere.

"She might not even want to come when she finds out it's with me," I whispered to Mother.

"Hileena Devi," Mother said, "it is true that our daughters are the fastest and the strongest in the village, but I do not see Anula here. You and I lost our husbands in the same war, and now both our sons have been taken. I am glad you feel as I do, and we gladly accept your offer, but for such a dangerous mission, surely Anula must choose to go of her own free will. Talk to her tonight and, if she agrees, meet us here at dawn. We must go now, for there is much to prepare."

Diipundi hesitated. "Your decisions have been made in haste. Consider it all again, then if you still decide to go ahead, prepare food for several days for your daughters to take. Then be ready to leave at first light. I will give them directions. There is no time to lose."

***

The night passed slowly. After cooking, eating, and packing some food into a back sling, I hardly slept at all. Finally, Mother, Seera and I were on our way back to Diipundi. We walked quickly and quietly. The cool darkness of the night still hid us, but when a rooster call joined the cawing of early scavenging crows, I knew that our cover was starting to lift. And lift it did.

A loud yelp announced us to the world. Seera, not seeing a sleeping dog in the darkness, stood on its tail. I knew instantly that it was Limpy, with his unmistakable little bark. He must have followed us home last night.

"Shush, Limpy!" I ordered quietly, hoping to prevent any further attention.

Looking sorry and frightened by the shock, Seera clasped Mother's hand and we continued.

As we got closer, I felt strange, hurried, yet hoping we would never arrive. I was excited by the thought of what I was undertaking for Patish, and even glad of the opportunity to prove myself. But I was afraid of the danger, who wouldn't be? Most of all, I was afraid that I might fail.

We turned off the main path onto the track that led to The Circle. Diipundi was there waiting, a small bag in one hand, a bamboo staff in the other. "Good, we are all here," he said, looking further up the path.

I turned to see Anula and her mother arriving just behind us.

As we sat in a circle, Diipundi lost no time. "My dear Leeta and Anula, the task you are about to undertake is a risky one for two young women. If you are seen by soldiers or their spies, you could be punished for opposing the Word of the Prince. Beyond the villages, you will need to pass through the grassy plains and thick forests where dangerous beasts roam, and there is no clear path to follow. Lose your bearings and you may be lost for days before you find the way again if you ever do. Do you understand these dangers?"

Anula and I answered: "We do."

"Then rightly I call you women now even though you have yet to undergo your Ritual of Womanhood, for the courage you show proves your womanhood. For this, your mothers will pierce one ear for you now and save one for your Ritual Day."

He opened his bag and took out a small parcel that he unwrapped to reveal two beautiful circular earrings and a metal ear piercer. "Leeta, you may have the first honour, since you were the first to volunteer."

Surprised and a little afraid of the piercing, I closed my eyes and bowed my head. Mother knelt forward and picked up the ear piercer.

I braced myself and held Patish's Earthmother figurine between my thumb and fingers. I felt a sharp pain in my right ear lobe and Mother smiled. Diipundi gave one of the earrings to Mother. She passed it through my stinging ear, and I felt the strange sensation of it dangling by my neck.

"Leeta, may I suggest you tie your Earthmother bracelet around your ankle?" said Diipundi. "The Earthmother will then bless your running."

"Yes," said Seera. "I told you, Leeta, you are an Earthrunner!"

"Indeed, a true Earthrunner," agreed Diipundi.

"Anula, here," offered Seera, "you can borrow mine to tie around your ankle, too."

"Oh, thanks so much, Seera, but I just couldn't," said Anula with a glance to her mother. "It's too precious, your special gift from your brother. But thanks again. And I'm sure the Earthmother will bless my running too."

I watched Anula's mother pick up the ear piercer. Anula braced herself as her mother completed the piercing.

Diipundi produced her earring. "Anula, this earring is identical to Leeta's. It is from the same pair; in recognition of this great deed you are undertaking together. You have grown up separately as girls, but now you enter womanhood together as sisters."

Diipundi took out another small cloth-bound parcel and unwrapped it to reveal a circular clay object that he lay down next to him. He moved the oil lamp closer, exposing coloured markings on the cloth.

"This map will guide you to the Abode of the Purple Sage," he said, pointing to marks on the cloth as he went on. "Now, listen carefully and capture these instructions with your eyes and ears. Turn left through the plains towards the great Naked Mountain. Listen for the heavy pounding of rhinos, for they will be able to smell you. If you see one, climb the nearest tree, but, if there are no trees nearby, stand perfectly still as the rhino's sight is poor and from a distance it may mistake you for a tree. If it gets too close…"

He stopped, looked at Mother then back at us before going on. "Your only hope will be to hit it hard between the eyes with this bamboo staff." He passed the staff to Anula. "When you reach the foothills, beware. If you encounter a sloth bear, it may think you're a danger and attack. Roll yourself up with your face between your knees. Don't move, wait until it leaves."

"And what of tigers, Diipundi?" my voice quivered.

"Past the Monkey Temple is the start of dense forest where tigers roam. Take this sandalwood balm," he said, handing me a small ceramic jar. "Its scent will confuse a tiger's senses, but proceed with utmost caution. Move in complete silence between bamboo clumps, squeezing yourself in amongst the dense bamboo. They were planted to provide protection, for a tiger won't be able to reach you."

Seera's eyes fixed on me. She knew better than anyone the sheer terror I was feeling. I was glad when Diipundi reached the end of the map.

"Here," he said, pointing, "you will reach a bridge of tree roots. Once you cross, you will be in the land of the mountain people. You will soon feel their eyes watching you, but do not be afraid, they are a kind and gentle people. When you do find them, or rather, when they find you, you must show them this." He picked up the flat clay disc with markings that had been pressed in a spiral pattern, speaking gently as if to reveal their secret.

"There is no greater Wisdom in the heavens or on the earth than the Wisdom in our hearts, waiting to be found," he added. "This is the Wisdom Wheel that the Wise One gave me long ago. When you show it to the Mountain People, they will take you to the Abode of the Purple Sage. Keep it safe, for without this, they will not trust you or take you to the Abode. Your mission would be doomed."

It was time to go. I had been very brave until now, but, as we followed Diipundi's lead and stood up, I felt sick in my stomach.

Seera looked at me, about to cry. Without a word, I embraced her. I felt her tears roll onto my shoulder dampening my drape.

Mother pulled me close. I wrapped my arms tightly around her, her arms equally as tight around me. I didn't ever want to let go.

"No matter what happens, Leeta, I will love you always," she promised, wiping her eyes with the back of her hand. "Forever. And Leeta, always put your safety first, always, even if it means you can't reach the Sage." She took a deep breath to give me one last blessing. "May the Wind fill your heart with courage, may the Earth give you strength with every step you take, and may the Sun lift your spirit so you can rise above every challenge on your path."

I gave Mother and Seera one last smile, and nodded loyally to Diipundi, who pressed his palms together and then brought them to his heart. His hands separated in a sweeping motion, the left palm open and pointing down to the earth, the right palm held firmly upwards. "Go."

I turned and ran, fists clenched.

"When you run," Diipundi had once said, teaching us the ideals of Earthrunning, "with every stride you take, feel your feet kissing Earthmother." I thought of Patish's feet on this dirt not long ago. The thought of kissing the earth tenderly with my feet suddenly had even more meaning.

I glanced over my shoulder. Anula was a breath behind. Like me, she'd tied her long yellow drape up and around her waist, freeing her legs below the knee as we did when we worked in the fields. Her fists were clenched into tight little balls, thin mouth pursed. She met my gaze and ran harder.

The stars had faded into the soft morning light. It was just enough to see the stretch of empty fields beside us. I could feel the dryness of the soil as it waited here for water, helpless. It seemed long ago that the tilling had been finished and seeding wouldn't begin until the first sign of rain. So far, there hadn't even been the first sign of clouds.

Chapter 4: Another Option?

Patish

I never entered a real sleep. My eyes were closed, but I kept thinking about what had happened. Now, with the first caw of a crow, I opened my eyelids to the soft pink light in the morning sky. It almost felt as if I were home, waking up outside where I often slept on hot nights. But it wasn't. Sounds of the camp spoke of my new reality.

When we'd camped down, I was too exhausted to look around, and, with no moon, I couldn't see far. But a few flaming torches revealed that we had joined up with a bigger group – probably men and boys from other villages in the valley. There were seven villages, so there would be three or four hundred of us altogether.

Sleeping bodies covered the ground, but a few started rising for their morning ablutions. Someone was lighting a fire near a clearing where horses, bullocks and a few carts stood. It reminded me of our valley's Festival of Games where we went to celebrate the harvest and test our strength against the other villagers. But where were the cries of hungry babies, and the squeals of young children playing?

"Is it morning already?" Satu said, sitting up. "It feels like I just went to sleep!"

The sound of his voice put me at ease. I wasn't alone, my soul brother was there too. Satu was more a brother than a friend. We had played together since we were toddlers while our mothers worked in the fields. As we grew, we became inseparable, and even though we were friends with all the village boys, our friendship always came first.

A strange thought came to me. How had I never thought about it before? Leeta was often with us when we were little. Did Satu and I leave her out as we grew? Or did it happen after Seera was born and she bonded to Leeta? Maybe I was making too much of it, but Leeta's disappointment with me at yesterday's monkey chase left me wondering.

Here with Satu and our sleeping friends, I realised that I was actually glad to be with them. Of course, I resented being taken, but I was glad we were all together. It would have been strange to be left behind. I felt guilty thinking how Mother would react if she knew.

Tomay and Sujas woke and looked around, still half asleep, while Liddu lay still, in a deep slumber.

"You four," a voice shouted, "get up and collect firewood for the cooks. Come on, move!" The owner of the voice, a big soldier who looked like his whole body was swollen and about to burst out of the tight garments he wore, gave Liddu a slight kick in the ribs, adding: "And take this lazy one with you."

We jumped to our feet. We knew this was the only response in the army. Compliance. I helped Liddu up, but I hid my annoyance at the soldier's brutish treatment. His eyes scrutinised us. Things were different now. I would have to learn to obey orders, and quickly. Orders are orders.

Without a word, we walked towards the carts where the morning meal was being prepared. I was still annoyed. That wasn't how decent people treated each other. Not in Shaktin, anyway.

As a child, I was always treated with adoration and respect. Our whole village was like one big family, connected by our guiding Way of the Heart. Diipundi, the village elder, was a living Master of The Way, having learnt directly from the Purple Sage. Other villages of the valley had elders like Diipundi, too, but most of them were so old they were losing their influence. Of course, not everyone in the village believed in The Way like we did. Some even ignored it, like Rakti and his sister, Anula. I remember when they returned to Shaktin about a year ago. We invited Rakti for a game of Kabaddi, but he just laughed at us. "Not interested," he'd said. We thought it was because they had lived in Taxila and they were city people now, too good for the village ways. Not that we really cared, but they always had an air of superiority, like we were inferiors. A bit like the way the soldier had just treated us.

"Great, our first job as soldiers – collecting firewood!" said Tomay, always ready for a joke. "He must know my mother."

"Well, could have been worse... manure patties, for example," quipped Satu loudly, motioning over to a group of boys heading off towards the horses and bullocks.

One of them, a solidly built boy named Vinto I recognised from Rolpur, a neighbouring village, overheard and called out in response. "Why, if it's not those nature-loving Shaktin peasants!" He ran back to the soldier who had given us the command and asked: "Sir, they love animals so much they would like to swap. And they're really good at making dung patties, that's what they do best!"

"Why, they're the dung patty champions of the valley, Sir!" quipped Solti, one of his friends.

All of them broke out in mocking laughter.

"Oh, is that so? Very well, you lot collect firewood and you lot, down to the animals," ordered the soldier, enjoying the laughter.

Our two groups looked at each other as we moved apart to follow the new orders.

"Thanks, Satu!" Sujas teased. "Of all the people in the camp, you had to choose Vinto to upset on our very first day."

"Don't blame me, I only opened a door," replied Satu. "Blame the thief who sneaked inside!"

"Well, we are pretty good at making dung patties," I jested. "But our chance will come to pay them back. Those Rolpur boys don't know what they've started."

"Don't know if we want to be making enemies in our own camp," Satu said. "We'll have enough enemies to deal with on the battlefield."

The word "enemies" stuck in my mind. I never thought I had an enemy, though Vinto and Solti had come pretty close to it at the festival last year.

After a breakfast of cracked wheat gruel, we marched without a break until the sun was directly above. Stopping for a rest in a mango grove, I checked the branches, but the mangoes had already been picked. It was hotter here and the mangoes ripened earlier than high up in the valley. We had no choice but to be content with the only thing the trees could offer: shade.

Exhausted, hot, and dehydrated, we dropped our packs then plunked down with them. Too tired to talk, I lay down and let my eyelids shut out the rest of the world. We had been promised a sleep in the high heat of the day. This was it, and I slept.

***

Everyone was lining up in front of some big baskets, so we joined the queue. Flatbread and a chickpea ball never tasted so good, and, when I washed it down with cold water from the long neck of the jug that was being passed around, I felt a bit more like myself.

"Have you ever been this far from Shaktin?" asked Liddu, not really asking anyone in particular. We were sitting with the boys from our village, waiting for the order to start marching again.

"I have – I've even been to Taxila," said Tomay, pointing into the distance.

The march had brought us right down through the valley to a view of the plains covered with fields. But further in the direction where Tomay's finger pointed, earthen shapes and towers rose out of the ground.

"And of course, so has Rakti – hey, Rakti," Tomay called to another group nearby.

Rakti turned towards us.

"Why don't you tell us about life in Taxila?" Tomay asked him.

"Yeah, tell us about the prince," said Liddu, always keen to hear a yarn.

Rakti smiled and came over to our group. "Before we returned to Shaktin, we lived in Taxila," he said, "just near the palace. I even got to go inside the palace sometimes to help Mother. She worked there as a decorator."

There was something about Rakti that made me feel uneasy. Maybe it was the way he never looked directly at you when he spoke.

"Why did you ever leave?" Liddu begged, mouth wide open. "It must have been amazing to go into the palace!"

"When Grandfather died, Mother was the only one who could take care of Grandmother, so we had to come back to the village," he said.

The way he said "back to the village" made it sound like the end of the earth. I thought he didn't like us, but now I wondered if he missed his life in Taxila. I would miss Shaktin terribly if I had to leave.

"You might get to see some of your old friends when we join the main camp," I said, hoping he might get back to the topic of the palace.

The palace held a fascination for all of us, and stories of its wealth and size abounded. Huge rooms that kept cool even in the hottest weather, clay pots big enough to stand in, and gardens full of beautiful exotic flowers and fruit trees. Even more fascinating was the fact that a young prince now ruled.

"Have you ever seen the prince?" Sujas asked.

Everyone stopped to listen.

A small smile indented Rakti's cheeks. "As a matter of fact, I once saved his life…"

Everyone stared.

"What?" said Satu. "You saved the prince's life and you're here, with us? Surely, he would have rewarded you?"

"He was only young at the time," explained Rakti, gazing down at his feet.

"Tell us!" pleaded Liddu.

"Well, one day, Mother was painting patterns on a garden table in the palace gardens. I was bringing her some more colours and brushes when I heard a frightened scream, 'Snake!' I dropped the paints and ran to where the voice had come from. There stood the young prince, frozen with fear against a wall. A huge cobra had him in a trance and was poised to strike. Without thinking of my own safety, I ran across and dived, grabbing its hooded neck with my bare hands. The prince was so thankful he said he would reward me with anything I wanted."

"Amazing!" said Liddu. "So, what did you ask for?"

"I had no idea. I looked around to see if there was anything I wanted, and my eyes fell on a white stallion tethered with some other horses nearby. It was such a beautiful beast, and its saddle was studded with jewels that sparkled so bright they could blind an enemy. I asked if I could ride it. The prince told me its name was Cloud. When I rode it, Cloud did everything I commanded."

"You should have asked for gold – lots of it!" cried Liddu.

Rakti glanced around the group. "That's what Mother said afterwards. But I'm sure that, if I ever need something, the prince would grant it with pleasure. And even if I didn't want to fight in this war, he would probably make me one of his palace guards. They don't really fight in the battles."

"So, you grabbed a live cobra with your bare hands?" questioned Satu.

"It was the biggest one I've ever seen! About four times the length of me."

"Cobras don't grow that big!" Satu scoffed.

"Are you accusing me of lying?" Rakti frowned.

"Not at all, Rakti," I butted in, "Satu is only trying to find out what to do if he was ever in such a predicament. Tell us how you handled it."

Satu just shook his head.

"That's a very good point, Patish," continued Rakti. "After all, it's not like I had ever caught one before! Luckily a guard appeared quickly and brought a basket with a lid. I had to drop it in such a way so that it couldn't bite me. Like this…" and he motioned with his hands as if to throw an imaginary huge cobra down into a basket.

"But its tail would be…" Satu objected.

I gave him a small nudge in the leg. Our eyes met and I frowned slightly, until he nodded as if he'd caught on.

To calm Rakti, I spoke quickly. "Yes, the tail of the horse, was it beautifully combed and platted? That's what we've heard, haven't we, Satu, that the prince's horse has a platted mane and tail."

"I think it might have been platted, yes, now I remember," nodded Rakti.

A loud conch ended the break. It was the signal to line up ready for marching. Rakti rejoined his friends as we picked up our packs and rose to our feet.

When we started to march, Satu moved close to me. "What's in that scheming head of yours, Patish? I know… you're just wanting to bait him for a bigger occasion, so that we can have a better laugh, right?"

That wasn't what I had in mind. "I know Rakti was bragging, but what if there is just a bit of truth in his story? I don't mean the snake part, but he has lived in Taxila, and his mother has worked in the palace – at least we know that's true. What if… suppose he does have some connections, obviously not the prince, but maybe someone high up?"

"Patish, what are you suggesting?"

"What if he really could get into the Palace Guard? What if he could get us in, too? You heard him – the Palace Guard don't fight in the battles."

Satu's face contorted. "What are you saying? Don't tell me you're afraid!"

I was stunned – my closest friend, the one I admired and trusted more than anyone, thought I was being a coward. "It's not like that, Satu. It's just... different. Last night I woke with really horrible thoughts that shook my soul. It's the reality of what's happening to us. Like what happened to Father. In a way, you're right, I was afraid of something. But not afraid to fight, not even afraid to die. I mean, well, afraid of dying because it would leave Mother and my sisters alone. Satu, I felt terrified, confused, ashamed, all at the same time. Mother's last words to me were a plea to survive, no matter what. No matter what."

I expected him to understand, but all he could say was "When the storm approaches, the ants flee for cover."

All he ever talked about was bravery and honour.

"It's alright for you, you've still got your Father!" I said bursting with anger.

I couldn't believe what he had said. I couldn't believe what I had said. Our feet kept walking, pounding the dirt and grass and twigs, and any unfortunate crawly thing that happened to be in our path. Confusion wiped out every feeling of warmth and connection we felt, not only for each other, but for anyone and anything at all.

The rest of the march continued in silence, a long, hot, dry silence. Satu was now ahead of me, next to Tomay. Had he moved away, or had I dropped behind? We kept marching in the unforgiving heat of the afternoon sun. I looked up in the hope of a bit of shade from a passing cloud, then down, knowing that the only cloud around was the dark storm cloud over our friendship.

Chapter 5: Limpy, the Three-Legged Dog

Leeta

"Limpy!" I gasped, hearing a dog panting behind me. I turned suddenly as he crashed into my legs. We nearly toppled over, but he didn't seem to mind. His long pink tongue flopped out of his mouth, baring his teeth, almost smiling. I grinned in return. "You gave me a fright," I told him.

He wagged his tail. We ran together until we reached Anula, who stood waiting for me. For a three-legged dog, he ran pretty well.

"I didn't know you were bringing him," Anula said, running again.

"I didn't 'bring' him, he just followed us. He does that all the time."

I ran level with Anula who picked up the pace. It felt like I was flying through the air, the anger from last night propelling me forward, the dry fields whirling past. With the Earth Shrine in sight, we ran neck and neck until the last moment when I reached out to touch it as Anula did too. We tapped the wall at the same time and came to a halt. Limpy arrived, panting heavily.

A smile lingered at the edge of Anula's lips as she stood catching her breath beside the rock-solid Shrine. It was a divine creation, carved by our ancestors with painstaking care into a small domed temple that stood with authority at the start of our village lands. Figurines in relief covered the outer walls, telling the story of the first peoples of our village, and of the oxen that were a part of our daily lives.

Anula saw me looking, then, with hands on hips, turned her back on the Shrine to look out across the path. My cheeks reddened. It was an obvious insult to our Way, an offence she'd never have dared if there were adults present.

"What are you doing?" I demanded.

She shrugged. Limpy came over and licked my ankle.

"Never mind her," I murmured, patting his head.

I squatted, untied my back sling, and reached for the small

container of sandalwood ointment. I knelt at the front of the Shrine, careful of the offerings of red powder and dried jasmine flower buds that littered the floor of the alcove where a figure of Earthmother stood, her wide hips and full breasts a display of her creative power. A single oil burner was at her feet, bearing a wick with a flickering yellow flame. I removed the lid, rubbed some ointment onto my forehead and bowed my head. Silently I gave thanks to her as I had so many times before, but this time I was desperate for her grace. As if assuring me, a slight breeze swayed wisps of my hair around my eyes.

I addressed the figure, "May the Earth protect me and guide me on this journey."

"Leeta?" Anula squatted beside me, scrunching her nose as if she had just inhaled the fragrance of fresh cow dung. "Do you really believe the Earthmother has any power? I mean..."

"Yes, I think she does. Do you want some ointment?"

I offered the clay container. Anula shook her head.

"Why do you care what I believe in, anyway?" I retorted.

"I was just asking," she shrugged. "It all seems kind of weird, the whole 'Earthmother' thing. I don't really get it."

"Well, I think your whole 'Ksanda' thing is even more weird!" I snapped. "That's probably why they're having a war – worshipping a warrior."

Anula raised her brows.

I held out the container. "Remember what Diipundi said about the ointment? It's the only protection we've got from tigers."

Anula rolled her eyes, ignoring my offering.

"Unless you think you can outrun one," I added, loud enough for her to hear.

"We're not going to be anywhere near tigers for days," she said, turning to her bag to avoid facing me. "I don't need your ointment, thanks."

Typical.

I turned back to the stone Earthmother. Her eyelids were half-open, as if she were slowly looking up at the world after a relaxation, and her full lips were slightly parted. The more I studied her peaceful expression, the surer I was that she had a real presence in the Shrine, and the power to guide me along this journey. And to give me the patience to deal with Anula's snide remarks. The small flickering flame at her feet almost died and then it burnt straight up again, strong and fiery. The conscripts – maybe even Patish – would have come to this point last night, and so I supposed they had lit it. They would have turned left here, as the path ended; we would go right.

Picking up my pack and slinging it over my shoulders, I readied to resume running. Anula immediately turned to me.

"We need to talk about the situation," she said.

I squinted in the sunlight. A fly buzzed, resting on Limpy's floppy ear that involuntarily flicked it away. "What situation?"

"The Limpy situation!" Anula declared. "We can't let him come. It's too dangerous."

Limpy looked up at us after hearing his name. How could he be dangerous? I doubted he'd ever hurt a fly. He seemed to spend most of his time in the village playing with the younger children or looking for a snack.

"I don't know what you're on about," I said, speaking with authority. When it came to knowledge of animals, I had learnt a lot from Mother. "Limpy could be a protector, even."

"Limpy, a protector?" Anula scoffed. "Limpy's clumsy and stupid!"

"Limpy's not stupid!" I said. "Just because he can't talk doesn't mean he can't understand."

Anula faked a smile. "Leeta, don't go all 'nature girl' on me. We need to return him to Shaktin."

"But we can't afford –"

" – to risk this whole mission?" Anula's eyes widened with apprehension. "What choice do we have? I thought you were serious about this journey, Leeta?"

I faced Limpy, seriously considering her proposition. He was sitting on his tail, a little crooked with only three legs. It was true, he wasn't supposed to come along, but I didn't think I could handle another goodbye from Mother and Seera. And we would lose valuable time.

"Please," I said. "Let's just keep going. Limpy will be fine."

Anula opened her mouth to protest, but I was quicker: "Or... maybe we could just try shooing him off. He'll find his own way back to Shaktin."

"It won't work," Anula said firmly. "He'll just follow."

Limpy nudged the edge of my leg with his wet nose, then began to sniff along the ground, always hungry.

"Food!" I said. "We'll give him some of our food and run." I opened my bag to get him something. Anula didn't move. "You pick something, too," I said.

"This is a stupid idea," Anula muttered. But she took off her bag, looked through it and held up a tiny piece of her flatbread. "On my count," she said, "we throw the food and run."

"One," I started, not letting Anula always take the lead.

"Two," she interjected.

"Three!"

We threw our pieces of bread as far as we could and broke into a run. When we reached a large neem tree, we stopped in its shade.

"I knew it," Anula said, looking back along the path. A small dark figure was running towards us.

"How did he eat that food so quickly?" I said.

Anula shrugged. "Limpy's a champion eater. He'd finish all the food in Shaktin if we let him."

As if understanding Anula's backhanded compliment, Limpy bypassed her and jumped up to lick my cheek as I bent down to pat him. I couldn't help but smile and gently pushed him away.

"That's only because he's starving half the time," I said. "Maybe if everyone in the village fed him a little bit more, he wouldn't scavenge so much."

"I knew the stupid food thing wouldn't work," she said. "We just have to take him back to Shaktin."

"Fine! You take him back then." Pulling my pack high onto my shoulders, I marched off along the narrowing track. Hearing no footsteps, I peeped over my shoulder. Anula was standing in the same position, arms crossed. This mission would be nearly impossible on my own, but I continued to walk, hoping Anula would follow. However, irritating as she was, her companionship was better than none.

"Leeta... fine." Anula walked briskly towards me. "Have it your way. But if anything happens because of Limpy, it will be your fault. Got it?"

***

The rest of the morning was long and gruelling. As we ran, I couldn't stop myself from being drawn back to the moment when Patish was taken from us, or the look in Mother's eyes when she let me go. Anula was quiet, too.

At last, we reached the great wild fig tree of the plateau. It was a giant, and I wondered how such a huge creature survived in this barren place. Diipundi had said some people called it the Tree of Hope.

"We turn left at the tree," I said, slowing to a walk as we approached. "It's kind of magical, isn't it?"

"Haven't you ever seen one before?"

"No, not this big," I said.

The closer we got, the more I was in awe. If its trunk was hollow, it would have easily fitted our hut inside it. It had massive limbs, thicker than Anula and me together, and roots like walls shoulder high where they met the trunk. Stepping close to it, I rested my hand upon its smooth surface to show it respect.

Then, I noticed something odd on the path ahead. "Anula! Get down, quick!" She spun around. "Get down!" I ordered.

"What is it?"

"Shush!"

Anula stepped to look out from behind the tree. She took a breath and then turned back to me. "It's a person?"

"A traveller, maybe?"

"Leeta, what if it's a spy? What if someone followed us from Shaktin?" She bit her bottom lip.

I hesitated. "But a spy would be hiding, not standing out in the open."

"Someone knows we're out here. What if they know what we're up to?"

"Let's just wait," I whispered. "He won't stand there forever."

Limpy started sniffing around in the grass.

"Limpy, get back here!" I whispered.

He kept moving away, so I went after him.

There, ahead of me in the grasses, was the dark figure of the stranger.

"Come here, Limpy!" I called. "Limpy! Stop!"

My mind raced. I could tell the stranger we had lost our way from the fields. Limpy turned his head for a moment, enjoying the fun of this chasey game. He paused just long enough for me to grab onto a handful of his thick fur. I stood up to face the stranger who I then saw had only half a face and was made entirely of wood.

"Greetings, Mister Spy," I burst out in laughter at the roughly sculptured, man-shaped pole. Although quite weathered, it had faint but clearly painted eyes and loose string for hair. The remains of a garment was tied around its waist.

Anula came up to me. "Why would anyone go to the trouble of putting this statue out here?"

"Maybe to mark the way?" I guessed.

"Well, we were very lucky it wasn't a spy. You must admit I was right, Leeta. Limpy could have got you killed."

I couldn't meet her eyes. "Well, he didn't. So, it's fine."

We took the opportunity to check our directions, carefully unfolding Diipundi's map. The next major landmark, the water hole, was still a long way off. We would be lucky to reach it by nightfall, and, without a path to follow, it almost felt like we were wandering aimlessly.

Wild grasses, waist high and pale yellow with dryness, grew in patches across the dusty land. I soon felt hot and thirsty. Running in this heat was tough. The dry terrain appeared endless, and the idea of a waterhole in such a landscape seemed bizarre. I tried my best to focus on the way my feet leapt across the dusty earth.

Limpy was keeping up, panting not far behind.

"Woah!" Anula cried, coming to a sudden halt. "There's another one of those man carvings!"

Sticking out above the grasses was another tall man pole, bearing similar weathered features to the previous one.

"That's creepy," said Anula, never afraid to ridicule. "Maybe there're people around and it's their deity. You know, a 'Lord of the Grasslands'."

Limpy growled, his tail shooting high into the air. Then he barked and raced towards a clearing where a pair of crows were pecking at something on the ground. The scavengers took off into the safety of the air, one of them holding something that dangled from its beak.

A brief mid-air tug of war followed, the crows fighting over the prize. As they flew above us, the object dropped, hitting Anula right across the face.

"Help!" she screamed in shock, rubbing her cheeks. A snake lay in front of her.

"A snake!" Anula thrust the bamboo staff into my hands. "Quick, kill it!"

"It's well and truly dead already," I said. "Look at how flat it is! Like someone has squashed it with a rock."

"*Cobras* have a flat hood," said Anula.

I wasn't sure if she had ever seen a cobra, having lived most her life in Taxila.

"Do you think there's someone crazy living out here?" she added, looking across the plains. "A snake-killing Lord of the Grasslands!"

"You know that's ridiculous!" I exclaimed, realising too late that she was mocking. "And you know you shouldn't call anyone 'crazy'. Anula, it's disrespectful."

She narrowed her eyes. "Like you can lecture me about respect after making fun of me and my belief in Ksanda this morning!"

"Well, what about you at the Shrine!"

"What just happened was a bad omen," she said. "I don't have a good feeling about this."

"A live snake falling on your face, now that would be a bad omen!" I grinned. "Or maybe just bad karma, you know, Lord of the Grasslands... Let's keep going."

"I'm serious," Anula said, her arms crossed over her chest. "Someone or something killed that snake, and you can bet it wasn't that weathered old excuse for a statue."

I took a deep breath. "We knew this was dangerous right from the start. The fact is that our brothers have been taken to fight in a war, a real war, with real killing and real dying. You can turn back if you want, but I'm going on with it. The Purple Sage is our only hope. I'm not giving up."

I held out the staff as an invitation. She took it without replying.

It was one thing to say I knew what I was doing, but deep in my belly was a hollow of doubt. I didn't know what dangers lay ahead, but I knew Diipundi wouldn't have warned us for nothing. Having Limpy with us felt good, like we were back in Shaktin, running for fun. Perhaps it was Earthmother's way of looking after us, but I wouldn't tell Anula that.

Chapter 6: Discipline

Patish

"This is where the battle will be," someone said.

The news spread along our lines and snapped me out of the monotony of marching all afternoon. A city of tents lay before us, but I knew that behind them lay the great Jhelum River. We couldn't see it from where we were, yet I longed to cool off in its water. And, on its other side, the Kingdom of Paurava. Our marching quickened.

"Halt!" came the order. "Rest while we wait."

What for? I didn't care, but seeing the army camp so close by drew me in. It stretched as far as my eye could reach, like a forest of people, more than I'd ever seen in any one place before.

Exhaustion and thirst brought me back to stand among long shadows of trees. Men gathered around a well and pulled up a bucket of water. As soon as it reached the surface, their hands and bowls dipped in. I longed to wash the dust from my throat and have a drink. Waiting my turn, I stood with Satu, Sujas, Tomay and Liddu, almost as if we were at the well of Shaktin. No one said much, though, and that made it clear. We weren't.

After a drink, I felt like I could talk again, but words weren't coming easily to my lips. Since my clash of anger with Satu, I didn't trust myself and chose to stay in the safety of silence.

"What are all the flags for?" Sujas asked.

We looked at the spread of soldiers. I hadn't particularly noticed the flags, but sure enough, above the various shelters and tents, there were flags of different shapes and colours. Deep in the middle were rows of tall narrow flags, their redness standing out from the dust floating around.

A bellowing shriek a bit like a conch captured our attention.

"Elephant!" said Tomay. "Imagine being an archer, riding high on its back," he said, drawing back the imaginary string of an imaginary bow and letting fly an imaginary arrow.

"I wonder how many there are?" said Liddu, excited. "Let's all join the elephant squad."

"Don't like your chances Liddu. You've never even ridden on an elephant!" said Satu.

"That's right," said a familiar voice.

It was Martal, and Sujas' father Pranava was with him. "I wouldn't expect to get into one of the elite squadrons if I were you. In fact, we'll probably all be split up soon into various units. Now listen to this." He whistled a little tune and Pranava joined in.

"Okay, boys, whistle it back," Pranava said.

It was a simple tune, and we whistled it without any problem.

"Memorise it," Pravana said. "Use it if you're looking for our villagers. It will be hard to find each other amongst all those soldiers once we're separated. There are many dangers in a camp even before the battle, and our best hope of survival is to help each other. Now practise it and pass it on."

I had no idea what dangers he was talking about, but I joined the others and did as we were told.

The whistling turned into a game with Sujas whistling, then all of us whistling back.

We stopped when we noticed a group of soldiers riding out towards us. They rode slowly, and every soldier nearby stood straight and saluted as they passed. They stopped nearby and dismounted, their horses attended to by a couple of soldiers who had been waiting.

The one in charge wore a deep red turban and a bronze armoured chest plate over a red and green gown. Soldiers greeted him while others hurried to form two straight lines on either side of him. As he walked slowly towards us, everyone stopped to stare. Around his waist, a wide leather belt carried a long-curved sword on his left hip, and, now that he was close to us, I could see a smaller dagger tucked in at the front, intricate carvings on its ivory handle. Maybe it had been a royal gift for some heroic act he had performed? His arms and legs were tight columns of muscles that rippled with every sharp, purposeful movement. A long, curled moustache almost covered his mouth, and matching bristly eyebrows protected his dark eye sockets that carried big, bulging eyeballs. So penetrating were his eyes, it wasn't hard to imagine an enemy being disarmed just by his look. He was everything I had imagined a general to be, a soldier, born to fight.

35

Without any command or signal, everyone stopped and stood to face this stunning leader. "I am Master Vinyak, servant of the Prince of Gandhara, and Commander of the Royal Army. You have come to serve your country at a time when we are threatened by the powerful army of Paurava."

His voice boomed across the field so everyone could hear him. Master Vinyak took a few measured steps sideways, eyes looking into ours one at a time, establishing a direct connection with every man and boy, the beginning of a loyalty that would see men lay down their lives at his command.

"The first and most important thing you must know is that an army relies on discipline for success. More than courage or any act of bravery or strength, it is discipline that will give an army its best results on the battlefield. And to have discipline on the battlefield, we must have discipline in training. You will now be placed under a unit commander who will be totally responsible for you, from your training right through to the first day of engagement with the enemy. I expect your total loyalty to your commander. His word will be your mission."

He stood still and stared at us as if he were looking into each individual's eyes, all at the same time.

"Any indiscipline will be answerable to me."

The silence was total. Not a man nor a boy nor a horse, nor even a bird, dared make a sound.

"Unit commanders, take over."

Without pause, one of the soldiers to his right stepped forward. He was the youngest real soldier that I had seen, and all the boys looked at him in awe, wondering how one so young could be a commander. I glanced at my friends and tried to guess what they were thinking. I had barely spoken to them since my painful words with Satu, and I wondered if Satu told anyone about it.

"I am Commander Rixten. All boys aged sixteen or under will be joining my unit, so make two lines by that tree," he ordered, pointing. His young soft voice sounded more like a plea, not like the thundering commands of the Master.

I picked up my pack and started walking to the tree with the others, noticing Asten bid goodbye to his father and join us. Other fathers and brothers broke into murmurs as they farewelled their youngest, but few of them actually moved.

The young commander seemed frustrated by this. He glanced momentarily at Master Vinyak, then, at the top of his boyish voice, he shouted: "I said all of those under sixteen years old, line up now!"

A few more boys moved to join the line, but some just continued in conversation. His cheeks turned red.

A group of boys around Vinto and Solti seemed to have noticed his frustration and were whispering and giggling, casting glances at him, almost challenging him to control them. So intent were they in this game that they failed to notice Master Vinyak step forward, his sharp eyes fixed on them and their antics.

"Line up as ordered!" his voice boomed, "Except for you…" and he pointed to Vinto and his friends, "Come here now!"

The smirks and smiles disappeared instantly from Vinto and his friends. They walked towards Master Vinyak. The other boys joined our line. The young commander regained some confidence and moved to a position at the front of his lines of young soldiers.

Master Vinyak lost no time with the boys standing nervously before him.

"Remove your tops," he ordered, then he walked purposefully to his horse. He reached up to the saddle and took a leather whip off a hook. He marched back, the coiled whip like an extension of his hand.

"You," he said, pointing to Vinto. "Step forward. Face the conscripts whom you have let down with your disgraceful behaviour."

Vinto turned to face the crowd, most of whom had no idea why he was about to be punished. He was well known in the valley after winning the final race at the recent Valley Games, but whatever respect that had earned him was tarnished by his reputation as a practical joker who would take any opportunity to have a laugh at anyone's expense. Now, the usual mischievous glint in his eyes was gone. This proud young prankster was shocked, standing bare chested, humiliated and about to taste the sting of the commander's whip.

Master Vinyak commanded: "Raise your hands up high. You are about to meet Discipline."

He unfurled the whip with a slight flick of his wrist. Like a serpent, the long leather whip lay in front of him in the dust, its thick handle firmly in his grip. With a sudden jerking motion of his arm, the thing came to life, flying high into the air behind him with a hiss, then with another flick, it raced forward with lightning speed to smack against Vinto's bare back. The sickening thlump cut through the silence and every muscle in my body tensed.

Vinto winced, his whole face contorted, but he kept his hands raised high. He had barely taken a breath when again Master Vinyak's arm sprung into motion and the vicious whip flew back before darting forward to strike again. This time, Vinto cried out in pain and fell to his knees, head arched back as trickles of bright red blood flowed down onto the pale cotton wrap around his waist.

"Next, arms in the air," Master Vinyak continued, with no anger, no sympathy, but a fully concentrated execution of action. Not a person spoke as one by one the other four boys of Rolpur stood up to taste the sting of Discipline. None could repeat Vinto's feat of silence after the first bite of the whip, and their anguished cries pained my ears. The lesson completed, Master Vinyak rolled Discipline back into a coil and stood to address the assembly.

"When a commander speaks, listen. Then do. Your lives, the lives of your comrades, and the success of the Royal Army of Gandhara depend on it."

Chapter 7: The Beast

Leeta

"Hot, hot, hot, hot!" Anula jumped from one foot to another, as if creating a new kind of dance. "The earth is like hot coals! That's what the omen was!"

Limpy barked, prancing around us. Could his paws stand the heat? I stepped off my grassy patch and onto the dirt.

"Owww!" I was sure the soles of my feet were burning.

Anula and I exchanged quick, pained expressions. I spotted a shadow from a tall tuft of grass and quickly jumped onto it. Anula copied and ran to another patch, balancing on it with one leg. The tufts offered us cooler ground than the baking hot brown earth. Like a game, we were desperate to find the next one. Limpy loved it, limping madly alongside us, yelping and wagging his tail.

Squinting in the sunlight, I eyed a large, dead bush that offered a bigger circle of shade ahead. Anula spotted it too.

"First one to the shrub!" she challenged.

"Not fair, you're already ahead!" I cried, leaping as fast as I could from one patch of grass to another, determined to win the race.

Reaching first, I turned to Anula to boast but when I saw her expression, I stopped. Her jaw dropped; brown eyes widened. She was as still as a statue.

"An-"

"Shh!" Moving only her hand, Anula slowly placed a finger on her lips, motioning for me not to say anything. Her eyes fixed on something behind me.

Limpy, too, stared, his tail down between his legs. I craned my neck around, peeping out from behind the dead shrub. And then, despite Anula's warning of silence, I stumbled sideways and let out the slightest of gasps.

From the look in its eyes, it heard me – a rhino! Through the thin branches and dried leaves of the shrub, I could see its huge, pale mass and menacing horn stretching out from its face. I had no doubt that, with just a toss of its thick-set neck, it could rip a whole tree out of the ground.

Stand still like a tree, Diipundi had said.

There was no way I could do anything else, anyway. Fear stuck my feet to the earth.

"Leeta," Anula whispered, so lightly that I could barely hear her. Without moving my head, I looked to her from the corner of my eye.

Bit by bit, she lowered herself into a squatting position. She motioned with her hands for me to follow suit. I looked back toward the rhino and took a breath, but I couldn't move. I stood motionless, imagining what I might look like to this rhino. A tree stump? Or a pole person, a Lord of the Grasslands...

Afraid it might hear the thump of my heartbeat; I held my breath. The rhino relaxed its head and began munching the wild grasses. I exhaled – too quickly, for Limpy must have sensed my relief. He let out an excited little yelp, but to me it sounded so loud that even the monkeys back in Shaktin would have heard it.

This time, the rhino followed the prick of its ears, and with its tree-trunk legs, it moved curiously towards us. The earth shook with every step, then it halted.

If we were to have any chance against this beast, I had to gather myself. With a long shaky breath, I bent down and scooped Limpy into my arms, one hand under his tail and the other under his front legs. We couldn't risk another bark.

"Have the bamboo staff ready," I mouthed at Anula. "To hit it in the face."

Anula looked up towards the approaching rhino and then back to me, her eyes wide with terror.

"It doesn't have a face," she stuttered.

Limpy was really struggling now. He had never been an obedient dog.

"You know what I mean," I hissed back.

The rhino moved closer to us, its slow thumping footsteps matching the pounding drum of my heartbeat.

Limpy struggled in my arms, and I squeezed him tighter. Sweat broke out on my forehead but I was simultaneously hot and cold, like when I had been sick. What were we doing, relying on a dead waist-high plant to camouflage us and save our lives? The bush was barely standing. Its sparse leaves were curled, and its branches were as thin as fingers. But with no trees nearby, we had no choice.

I looked back to Anula. She had raised the bamboo staff above her shoulders, preparing for a strike at the rhino, but a telling tremor was visible in her arms. She met my eyes. For a moment, we connected. Her earring shimmered in the glare of the afternoon sunlight, and I felt mine, its twin, dangle against the edge of my jawline. Anula began to shake her head ever so slightly, as if trying to say, *I can't do this.* I gave her a long steady look but, as much as I tried to encourage her, I wasn't convinced myself.

The rhino halted right in front me. Trying not to gasp, I froze. Limpy stopped his struggle, intimidated by the giant animal only a step away. One single movement would send it charging into me.

There was nothing I could do to stop the sickness stirring in my stomach. The rhino, Limpy, the shrub... I couldn't focus on anything. Dizziness was taking over; the ground was spinning. I was losing control.

I felt an involuntarily clench in my stomach, and suddenly, vomit gushed out of my mouth, all over the right eye of the unsuspecting rhino. Shocked, it turned and bolted away. I slumped backwards onto the ground and Limpy fell from my arms.

The sound of the rhino's pounding steps retreating into the distance was more than a comforting balm for my shaking body. I tried to lift my head, but the world was still circling around me.

"It's okay, Leeta, the rhino has fled," Anula said. I closed my eyes. Had that really happened? "Great vomit, by the way."

I half-smiled and imagined telling the story to Patish and Seera.

"Don't look so glum – we could have been dead, you know," Anula said. "Although," she continued dryly, "I *was* ready to hit it with the bamboo, of course. I was just waiting for the right moment."

We'd made it with our lives – this time. I couldn't help but wonder if we would always be this lucky.

Chapter 8: New Friends

Patish

W e were last to arrive, far behind the rest. They had already disappeared among the tents and soldiers. I held Solti with one arm under his armpit, his other arm over my shoulder. He could barely walk, wincing with every step he took. Satu and I had stepped forward to help when Commander Rixten asked for volunteers. Sujas, Tomay, and Asten followed to support the other wounded boys, while Liddu carried their packs.

Strange how our first lesson on discipline had united us with the Rolpur boys. Our rivalry vanished; the whipping changed our perspective. Past and personal reputations no longer counted. In the army, we were all the same, and all that counted was our ability to listen to orders and carry them out. That's what Martal had been talking about; we would need to support each other more than ever. But allegiance to friends could also be disastrous. As the Rolpur boys had just found out.

Two young soldiers in brown waist wraps and red tops, the uniform of the Gandharan army, were allocating us to squad tents. At their feet were baskets of red cloths, and one of them held a rope with bundles of coloured strips tied to it.

"Your village and your name," ordered the one holding the rope.

"I am Satu of Shaktin, and these are..."

"I didn't ask you for your friends' names! So, you're the Shaktin boys? And you lot," he said looking at the miserable ones we were supporting, "...you must be the Rolpur fools!" He laughed to himself and continued: "I'd be careful not to cross Master Vinyak again if I were you."

"So where do we go?"

For the first time, I could see a disturbed look on Satu's face. Was he was starting to see through the whole soldier thing?

"You'll go where I tell you. No way you Shaktin or Rolpur boys will stay together. You, the tent behind the triangular green flag." He pulled loose a green strip of cloth and handed it to Satu. "Your headband."

"And here is your uniform," said the other, handing him a folded red cloth.

Satu turned to us, but avoided my gaze. "I guess I'll be seeing you around... and don't forget what Martal said."

The war hadn't even started, and I'd already lost my family, my village, and my best friend.

Our tents weren't far apart, and I could see the one I had been assigned to, in the third row behind the green flag, a canopy of cotton sheeting over a frame of bamboo poles. Red uniform and green headband in hand, I approached the opening just as three boys were coming out.

"Are you in here, too?" one of them asked.

"There's not much space left," said another. Straw mats, sheets and packs covered every bit of the floor space. "But we'll make some room for you later. We're going to take a bath in the river... why don't you come with us?"

His friendliness took me by surprise, a welcome contrast to the soldiers I'd met so far.

"Okay, I need to shed this skin of dust I've grown," I said, trying a bit of humour.

"You look like you've just crawled out of the earth!" he responded.

They watched as I put my pack and uniform down. I took out a clean waist wrap, picked up the red uniform, and stood to face him.

"Patish is my name, I'm from Shaktin. And you?"

"I'm Laksa," he replied, "and this is Janam and Talbik. We're from Jalnat, the next village down the river."

We stepped outside and I looked over the collection of hundreds of tents that made up this new home. We were at a slightly higher spot than most and started walking down the gentle slope. I looked across towards the row of trees where we were heading and saw a large gap, then much further away, what seemed to be another distant camp of tents.

"That's the Pauravan camp on the other side of the river Jhelum, or what there is of it at the moment," commented Laksa.

"And we'll be giving them a good lesson soon," added Talbik.

"Shaktin, I've heard of that before," said Janam. "Isn't it one of those Earthmother goddess worshipping villages?"

I felt uneasy. Laksa and Talbik could have been looking at a leper, or a Pauravan. Distrust. I'd seen it several times before. Like the last Valley Festival, when the Rolpur boys had been really nasty. Vinto spat on the ground to make mud for us to roll in, implying we were like pigs because we were nature lovers. It almost ended in a fight.

"It's not exactly like that," I said. I didn't want to lose their friendship; I was part of this group now. "We're not really worshipping any goddess, it's just a way of looking at things, you know... life, death... and it's not like everyone in the whole village is the same about it either. Our village elder Diipundi often talks about things, and he makes sense. He learnt directly from the Purple Sage, and that's where a lot of our Earthmother nature ideas come from."

"Is it true that the Purple Sage brought the champion warrior Siltek back to life after he'd been slain by an arrow through his heart?" asked Laksa.

Before I could answer, the others asked their own questions.

"Has Diipundi got any magic potions from the Purple Sage?"

"Have you ever seen the Purple Sage?"

"If Mother Nature is so strong, why can't she send enough water so we wouldn't need a war in the first place!" quipped Janam.

"I've only heard stories like you have," I answered, to be agreeable. "Hey, look at the archers!"

A line of archers in the middle of a drill stood side on, long bows at the end of outstretched arms; together they pulled back their arrows until their hands were beside their ears.

"Shoot!" came the order.

The missiles whistled through the air and whammed into a fallen tree trunk that served as the target. The archers then dropped to their knees as another row behind them parted their legs in the same firm stance, pulled back their arrows and waited a moment for the command.

"Shoot!"

Instantly their strings twanged. Again, the arrows thudded into

44

the soft wood already studded with the previous arrows. It was the end of the drill and, as the archers collected their arrows, we were in awe of their killing power.

"I'd like to be an archer!" said Talbik.

"I don't think so," said Laksa as we resumed our walk through the camp towards the river. "It's a lot harder than it looks," he added with authority. "My uncle is an archer, and I couldn't even pull back the string on his bow… that was a couple of years ago when I was younger. We'll probably be lancers. That's the easiest, you just thrust the spear into the heart of the enemy, like this…" and he motioned with both hands as his bent leg thrust forward, adding his body weight to the power of an imaginary thrust.

"Lancers?" I asked. "Aren't they at the front when a battle begins?"

"That's right – we get the first chance to be heroes," answered Laksa.

I knew I'd better not say what I was really thinking.

I was fascinated by everything I saw in the busy camp. It was different from what I had imagined, and much bigger. I had pictured all the soldiers doing everything at the same time, one big mass of soldiers in rows, all wearing exactly the same uniform, all practising the same drills. But here there was chaos, soldiers relaxing near tents, others wrestling, a group swinging bamboo staffs, individuals and groups walking to and fro in all directions. Even the uniforms were varied, like the men who wore them. Slim young bodies and burly bearded ones, some with metal swords and spear heads, and circular metal shields that glittered in the late sun – all part of one big commotion. I realised that thousands of soldiers couldn't have a bath at the same time, eat, train, or do anything as one big group. But in the end, they would be a single unit when the real battle began.

We walked on, past men coming back from the river in clean clothing, hair glistening wet, carrying washed clothes in their hands. I caught a waft of coconut oil in the air. "Medicine for parched skin," Diipundi would say, but I didn't have any. I was surprised at how relaxed the atmosphere was. Soldiers stood talking, while others sat, laughing. Further on we passed a group of angry, raised voices. An argument was brewing, so we hastened away.

A row of fires was being lit and the smoke from burning cow dung patties reached our nostrils as a group of men prepared for the evening meal. This hive of activity was obviously a kitchen, and I tried to imagine how much food would be required to feed the whole army. A cook cut a long marrow, squatting with one foot holding down the wooden base of his vegetable cutter, his hands moving back and forth, quickly reducing it to chunky pieces. Another squatted over a slab of stone, his hands crushing pieces of turmeric with a smooth rock. He scooped up the yellow pulp and put it with the other piles of spices he had already ground.

The closer I looked, the more I realised how methodical it all was. A team of potters took advantage of the setting sun, turning out an array of clay pots that they laid out ready for drying in the full heat of tomorrow's sun.

We finally reached the bank of the river. Most of the riverbed was dry, covered by smooth pebbles, so we continued until we reached the edge of a shallow rivulet running down the middle. All along, people bathed, washed clothing and stood around talking in the relaxed coolness that it offered. The water's width was about twenty steps, but only knee deep at its deepest. Many squatted or lay back in the refreshing water. From the other side, too, Pauravan men and women bathed, and I saw that a Pauravan village stood not far back, opposite us, almost hidden by the enormous army camp pitched around it. You would never have known that the people on each side were getting ready for war.

We put down our fresh clothing and waded in. The cool water was invigorating. When I reached the deepest part in the middle, I sensed I had gone far enough, not wanting to find myself amongst the Pauravan villagers or soldiers. I lowered myself to my knees then sat on the bottom, the water up to my shoulders. I stretched out and allowed myself to float on my back for a few moments. It felt like nirvana, floating freely in bliss. What a change; the water totally cleansed away every dry and bitter feeling that this wretched day had brought. I floated with eyes closed, enjoying the feeling of a smile on my face. My thoughts went to Seera, Leeta, and Mother. How I missed them.

Still floating, I felt my head hit soft flesh. I stood up and wiped away the water from my face to see who I had bumped into. "Sorry... I wasn't looking," I blurted out with some urgency as the long-haired figure turned to face me.

"I'm sorry, too," said a Pauravan girl, almost face to face with me. Her beauty startled me, before she looked away.

Shy, I thought as a slight but suppressed smile crossed her glistening lips. I stood speechless, stunned.

"Be off and look where you're going next time!" called a stern voice belonging to a young Pauravan man wading towards me.

"It was just as much my fault, but he's already apologised," the girl said, turning to face him. She turned her head back to give me one more glance before stepping directly into his path.

"We'll be meeting soon enough in battle," he cried, his angry eyes fixed on me.

The girl looked back at me, then faced him defiantly. "That's a terrible thing to say... apologise, or I'm telling Mother!"

Laksa had been watching and he ran up to me, splashing as he went. "Pauravan threatening you? Thinks he owns the river, does he?"

"It's alright," I said, as Janam and Talbik hurried to us, keen to get involved. I smiled at the girl and the young man, nodding my head, "Everything is fine, it was all my fault... I wasn't looking. Sorry again." I turned back to Laksa and the others, "Come, let's go, must be getting close to mealtime."

We waded back towards our clothing as the topic of conversation turned to food. I felt relieved that the tension was over, but I couldn't help thinking of the girl and the conversation I might have had free of the lurking darkness of war.

"I wonder what they're cooking for dinner?" Janam said.

"I'm starving after our long march," I added, trying to get back into the conversation.

"Well, if it's as good as the meal we had at lunch, you'll be able to have as much as you like," joked Laksa.

"Why, what was it?"

"Bits'n'pieces stew, without the pieces," Talbik grimaced.

"There were so many scraps even the dogs and the pigs couldn't eat it all!" added Laksa, and they all laughed.

I liked this group because they didn't take things too seriously, a bit like Satu. I wondered where he was and who he had ended up with. I looked along the river almost expecting him to be there among the other bathers. But there was no Satu, or anyone else I knew. What would I say anyway? It was strange how difficult it was to know how to fix things with him. Our friendship was a part of me, and I couldn't imagine myself without it. I couldn't imagine myself without my nose either, but it was easier to imagine that than not having my friendship with Satu.

A glowing orange sun hung low in the sky as we reached our clean clothing. For the first time, I dressed in the red cloth of a soldier. I picked up my wet garments and joined the others scrubbing them against the pebbles.

"Back in Shaktin I'd have done this with a cup of water," I said to the boys.

Laksa, who was wringing his own cloths, looked sideways at me. "Oh, well, we've got water here, but we have to fight for it," he said.

"I don't really get it... there seems to be enough for everyone," I spoke with caution.

"You don't get it, do you?" Laksa said. "You will when you see the canal."

"Let's see how the canal digging is going," Janam suggested.

"Yeah, I wonder if they've finished it," said Talbik, wringing the last drop of water out of his cloth before throwing it over his shoulder.

"What's the canal?" I asked.

"It's what the war is all about," answered Laksa. "Come on, you'll see."

At the mention of war, I faced the reality of the situation again. Bathing had somehow soothed my spirit, but here I was, a soldier, preparing for war. We walked along the side of the river. For a war zone, I thought it was an especially peaceful place with a special beauty of its own. The river was like a vein that provided life-giving water to the villages on both sides of its banks, and to the animals and birds that came and left with little disturbance to anyone. Now it was also the lifeline for two armies preparing to kill each other in a battle for the water. I was continually amazed at just how big the camps on either side of the river were. I thought of the battle, of these men killing each other in this beautiful place. It didn't seem real, and it didn't seem right. A river red with blood could never be right.

Laksa turned towards a group of soldiers who looked at us as we approached. They were guards in full uniform, complete with leather belts and swords and coloured bands, which spoke of their roles and authority. Their weapons looked deadly, and the metal tipped spears they held as barriers clearly meant they had no intention of letting us through.

One of them, a sturdy older man, motioned gently with his turbaned head, as if to ask: "What do you want?" without uttering a word.

"We're just having a look at the canal. How close is it to being finished?" asked Laksa, sounding like he was talking to an old friend rather than being challenged by a guard. The guard looked at him for a moment then glanced sideways at the other guard, who stepped forward to answer.

"Can't speak," he said, with a slight nod towards the older soldier, "Bit his tongue off when an arrow hit him in the leg... must have hurt more than the arrow!"

The older guard nodded with a slight smile. His story had been told many times before. "Wasn't even in a war; it was a stray arrow from a novice during training. So, you boys must be new conscripts. They've picked young ones this time!"

We nodded in agreement.

"Have a look," the guard beckoned. "Probably ten to fifteen days to go."

"I saw it when our village worked on it in during the last moon," said Laksa. "We're from Jalnat, the second village down the river, and he's from Shaktin, the valley village..."

I braced myself, expecting a comment about Shaktin from the guard, but he just nodded and added "Don't touch the ropes.".

"They show the level of the water and that's how the diggers know how deep to make the canal," Laksa said, pointing to the tightly stretched rope that was attached to a series of bamboo poles staked out at intervals.

"See those big rocks over there?" he continued, pointing to a row of large rocks at the edge of the dry riverbed. "When the digging of the canal is finished, they'll move the rocks away from the edge to unblock the water and it will flow into the canal."

"Let's see where they're up to with the digging," said Janam.

We followed him.

I moved next to Laksa. "Thanks for not saying more about Shaktin before," I said.

"That's alright," he said. "I realised you probably don't want to be branded that way. I don't know why people make a big deal of it anyway."

I smiled and nodded. I liked Laksa.

We reached the start of the canal-in-making and stood amongst the freshly abandoned collection of digging tools and woven baskets used for carrying soil and stones. I examined it all with curiosity. This is what the war is about.

The canal was as long as the eye could see, like a trail of some gigantic snake. It was as wide as two men lying head to toe, and rocks and pebbles of various sizes had been taken from the riverbed to line its base, enticing the river's water. I could see its depth was lower than the riverbed so that when the digging reached the river's edge, it would divert virtually all the river's water. The thought of it caused me to gasp. The Pauravan villages down the river would have little or no water. Now for the first time I understood why they were preparing for war.

"Further down they're making small canals that will carry the water into fields for rice," said Laksa. "It will make our villages wealthy."

"What's rice?" I asked, wondering what could be worth a war.

"It's delicious, and much easier to cook than bread," Janam answered.

"And cooked with milk and honey it's like a nectar of the gods," added Laksa, licking his lips.

"Don't count on getting any here, though," Talbik said, backing up his previous comments about the camp food.

The talk of food reminded us of our hunger, and the smells of fire and cooking were enough to get us walking back to our base.

We arrived expecting to find a busy kitchen with delicious aromas like the ones we had just seen. It was anything but. A bunch of boys stood in the middle surrounded by pots and baskets of food, arguing over who would do what. No wonder Laksa, Janam and Talbik were ridiculing the food. Not many boys knew how to cook, and, even if they had helped with cooking at home like I had, it would be a whole different thing to cook for hundreds instead of a family.

***

"Food's ready."

In a large clearing near the kitchen, we sat in a long row, faces in the darkness. The Shaktin boys must be out there somewhere. I looked along the rows for the mischievous grin of Liddu, or the reassuring eyes of Satu, but it was too dark.

A group of boys slowly dragged a large round pot along the hungry line. Ahead of them a boy gave out pieces of banana leaf and someone used a long ladle to scoop a helping of thick, steaming stew onto my banana leaf. Another pair of boys followed with a basket full of huge flatbreads, giving one to every hand that reached out.

I used the last piece of my half-cooked bread to wipe the banana leaf clean of the stew that I enjoyed simply for its filling capacity. When I finished, I noticed cheering and laughter coming from nearby. Flaming torches could be seen twirling in the otherwise dark night.

"Flame dancers!" I heard.

"Let's go," said Laksa.

A troupe of six bare-topped men were twirling torches that left trails of glowing spots flying behind in great arcs. In a well-rehearsed motion, one of them leapt onto the bent knee of another, then up onto the shoulders of the biggest of them, a muscular man built like a rhino who grabbed his ankles and held tight. A smaller performer, aided by another, climbed them both to make a third tier. Balancing on the shoulders of the second performer, he caught two torches, one in each hand, and began juggling them to the spontaneous cheers and applause of the crowd. Up high and spinning, the cinders looked like galaxies of stars being cast across the darkness where they remained as twinkling points of light filling the otherwise black sky.

In all the excitement, I lost sight of Laksa and the others. A sea of unrecognisable faces surrounded me, waiting for the next performance.

A gentle drumbeat started, creating a wave of hush over the chatting. As it spread through the night air, another drum joined in, then rhythmic clapping started all around.

A loud penetrating voice joined the rhythm, strangely haunting yet comforting at the same time. At first, I wasn't sure if it was wailing or an ecstatic cry, but whatever it was, I had never heard so much raw emotion in a voice.

"Ahhhhh, ohhhhh, ooooooh, iiiihhhh…" then as it quietened for a moment, the voice burst into song.

> My heart won't cry, not a tear will drop,
> Til I walk upon the soil,
> Of home…

Like a well-rehearsed choir, everyone joined in, repeating the verse, every voice full of the melancholy of men longing for their loved ones.

The lone voice again pierced the night, even more passionate than before.

> My eyes won't smile, not a tear will drop,
> til I look into your eyes,
> upon the soil,
> Of home…

The surge of voices swept us in, and I found myself singing too, my heart aching in the flow of song.

> My eyes won't smile, not a tear will drop,
> til I look into your eyes,
> upon the soil,
> Of home…

I closed my eyes. It felt as if we were in the Circle back home, the villagers singing as Diipundi led the call and response. Sometimes at celebrations we'd stay up all night waiting for the drummers to tire so we could take over, then sleep well into the day so we could do it again the next night.

As the song went on, in the short gaps of silence between verses, the last word or two kept drifting in late, like an echo coming from another distant group. At first, I thought it was from another part of the camp, perhaps beyond the canal, as the army was spread a long way down the river. I listened more intently. Even though my sense of direction had become disoriented in the darkness, I realised that our junior camp was behind me to my right, and I was facing in the direction of the rest of the camp along the river. The echo should be coming from in front of me. I listened even more intently, and the more I listened, the more it became clear that it was coming from my left, the direction of the river. Again, it came – this was an echo from another huge mass of singers. Could they be sitting on the riverbank? And who were they?

Perplexed, I stood and began making my way towards the river. It wasn't that easy. The soldiers were seated close to each other like a woven mat covering the earth, and for each step I had to find a gap to place my foot. Stepping carefully between them as they sang in waves, I moved toward the distant echo of song that continued to float in across the warm, still air of the night.

Eventually, I reached the outer perimeter of the singing army. Stepping freely, I walked towards the river, the singing behind me still loud but growing less so with every step I took, while the singing of the same song from in front of me grew gradually louder. I realised it could only be coming from one place – the other side of the river! As I reached the riverbank, a strange elation overcame me and I dropped to my knees, captivated by the waves of song coming from either side of the river. The strangeness of it all – was I dreaming? Two armies in preparation for battle yet singing together harmoniously like the villages in our valley during harvest celebrations.

The gentle flow of the river spoke to me of how for countless years She had listened to the villagers on both sides as they opened their hearts and told their stories in songs of the night, joining in the harmonies as one people. Here, where their kingdoms met, separated only by a narrow stretch of water, the Gandharans and Pauravans had bathed together after a hard day's toil. And even marriages between them were not uncommon. I thought again of the girl I had bumped into near this very spot and imagined how under normal circumstances friendships would have been formed. These people had more in common with each other than with other people of the very kingdoms to which they belonged. Gandhara and Paurava had been close friends for as long as anyone could remember. We spoke the same language and fought side by side in the last war. But now we were enemies.

How could this impending war be real? I sat down and pondered, alone between these two massive choirs. A spray of brilliant stars covered the sky. I recognised them as the same ones that decorated our Shaktin sky, and with them the first sliver of the newly growing moon. At least they were here, ever reliable celestial friends that would never desert me.

Chapter 9: Monkey Temple

Leeta

I woke to a warm wet tongue gliding over my face. His black eyes were staring hopefully into mine. They seemed to brighten at the sound of my voice.

"Limpy! What are you doing?"

"Look who decided to get up," Anula tittered when I emerged from the bark shelter, squinting in the morning sunlight. Everything came back quickly. The rhinoceros about to charge. Mother's tears. Patish being taken. Patish, taken. Anula was still talking. "You've been snoring for hours!"

I yawned and settled into a cross-legged position. Limpy immediately rested his chin onto my thigh, a ready-made headrest. I stroked the top of his head.

"Then why didn't you wake me? We'd planned to get up early and have a good start."

"I'm not your mother."

Limpy met my eyes. I raised my eyebrows to him as if to say *what's her problem?* He licked my fingers.

I looked up into the sky, an expanse of featureless blue. Water could save Patish and end this journey. I couldn't give up the hope for a beautiful, misty cloud – but the heavens remained bare.

After sharing some flatbread with Limpy, I stood holding my pack and hoisted it over my shoulder. Anula stood up brushing dirt off her yellow drape, determined to keep it clean. Her hair hung in a tight plait that rested on her shoulders.

"Okay, lead the way!" I said, nodding toward the forested hills before us.

We jogged silently with a few short breaks until we could bear the thrashing heat of the midday sun no longer and stopped for a longer rest alongside three great rocks. Each was big enough to lie on – if they hadn't been so hot to touch. We settled for their shade to sit in.

I untied my pack and pulled out the water gourd. After a sip of water, I took out the map and the sandalwood balm. I rubbed a little on my forehead and breathed in its protective fragrance. Soon, we would be in the forest, and we didn't need a tiger on our trail.

Tapping her finger on the map, Anula said, "What is this anyway? It doesn't help us much. We might get lost. How do we know we're not lost already?" She folded her arms across her chest.

"Once we reach the top of this hill, we'll see the Naked Mountain and move towards it," I said. It was logical.

"Yeah, but it doesn't mean that we're definitely going in the right direction…"

"We were at the water hole yesterday," I said, pointing defiantly to the little drawing of it. "And we've reached the foothills. So, we must be about… here."

"I don't know," Anula murmured. "I'm just feeling worried today. We're in the middle of nowhere, and anything could happen. There could be a predator about to attack at any moment!"

"I have hardly seen a single animal today," I interrupted. "We know the way back, so let's just keep going. We're doing fine. We really are." I wasn't sure who I was convincing.

"We were so close to that rhino yesterday," Anula shrugged, "I'm just scared it'll happen again. Aren't you?"

"Of course," I gulped. "Of course, I am."

Soon, we had the confirmation we were seeking. At the top of the hill, I caught my first glimpse of the Naked Mountain. There it stood, a marvel of rock jutting out from the earth to the heavens above. And naked it was – rock, pure and simple like a giant, muscular deity rising above the rest of the world, powerful and unhindered by the doings of people. We were approaching the realm of the Purple Sage.

I grinned and looked at Anula, but neither of us said a word.

We decided it was time for lunch. I settled under the shade of a tree and untied my bag. Limpy sensed a meal, and his wet nose nudged my leg with excitement. I threw him a piece of flatbread and turned back to the incredible view before us. And then, with a swipe so fast that I nearly missed it, Anula's lunch was snatched away.

"Oh, Earthmother!" I exclaimed. "What was *that*?"

"I didn't see that one coming," said Anula, still holding out her hand as a monkey sped up a tree with her bread.

Limpy raced around with excitement, yapping up at the treetops and trying to jump up to the little creatures.

"They're kind of cute," I said.

"Are you sure about that?" Anula pointed to a monkey dragging my pack away. It stopped and held up a stolen banana as its wide-eyed friends approached.

"Hey!" I warned, trying to get my things before they did.

One of the monkeys let out a sharp screech and another one joined in. The villains took off, dragging the pack along. "My food… and the map!"

We darted after them. Limpy barked madly from behind. I ran faster and reached for the pack, but one of the monkeys nipped my hand. "Ow!"

"Don't worry, I'll get it," Anula yelled, lunging forward and pinning the pack down with the bamboo staff. She hissed at the monkeys and pulled the pack away, holding it high above their jumping bodies. "Got it!" She relaxed for a second too long.

"Look out!" I cried.

She looked down. One of the bigger monkeys bit her ankle and she screamed. The pack landed with a thud and was immediately dragged away by the desperate little thieves. I grabbed the rope and the knife that had fallen out and watched them climb up into a tree, swinging away through the vines.

"Can you run?" I asked Anula as she rubbed her leg. "I mean, those tiny monkeys are pretty brutal…"

"Go – I'll catch up," she said.

With Limpy beside me, I picked up the bamboo staff and followed the shrieks of the monkeys. It was getting darker, almost eerie. The only sunlight was that which poured through gaps between the treetops. We were well and truly in the rainforest.

I slowed to a walk, trying to work out which direction the monkey shrieks were coming from. A curious little monkey in a tree caught my attention and I jumped uneasily towards it. For a moment, I thought it had a cloth headband on, but I lost sight of it. Could it be…?

I took a few more steps into a clearing where monkeys were everywhere. One of them held my pack. It wore a cloth headband – the bandage I had tied on it! It threw the pack down, and it landed a few steps away. I clasped my hands together in a sign of thanks and respect to the monkey and to Earthmother. "Anula, I have it!" I called, turning to see where she was. But I had spoken too soon, for a large monkey appeared out of nowhere, snatched the pack and scampered off safely among the other monkeys.

"Where is it?" Anula huffed.

"There are so many of them," I groaned. "I can't see it."

We slowly moved on and came to a small building with a domed roof supported by pillars covered with engravings. Monkeys surrounded the little building, sitting on the edge of the roof.

"The Monkey Temple!" I said. "We're going the right way."

The monkeys seemed to be guarding it, so I edged forward with caution. Anula waved to me and motioned toward the temple. My pack! It was on the ground in front of the temple, just in front of a frowning monkey. Despite the tremor in my hands, I stepped forward. Closer, closer. Limpy followed, his tail lowered between his legs.

"Monkey Jii," I said, summoning my most confident voice. "That's my pack you've got there, and we really need it." I looked into his eyes, pleading. I held out the staff.

"Leeta, I know you say you love animals and all, but really, this is a bit ridiculous."

I ignored her. "I'll tell you a secret, monkey friend."

The monkey cocked its head to one side like Limpy does when he's trying to understand. I lowered my voice. "We're on a mission, okay?" I was whispering now. "We just need you to help us."

I moved my foot carefully, slowly, without breaking eye contact with the monkey. Not looking where I placed my foot, I stepped on Limpy's tail – *AAWRRFFF*! He yelped with an ear-splitting screech, touched my foot with his snout then scampered away. I swooped swiftly and grabbed the pack.

"Go, go, go!" I cried.

We bolted deeper into the forest.

***

58

As night fell, every moment there was something – the crunching of a leaf, a flapping of wings, a hoot or a slither. At the slightest rustle nearby, we would react, and standing still wasn't an option because crawling insects would soon climb up our legs. Sleeping on the forest floor was also out of the question, so we climbed a nearby tree and used our drapes and rope to secure ourselves to the trunk while our legs lay across the main branches. Limpy was sniffing around at the base of the tree, and I could hear him scratching away before settling again.

"Do you think this is safe?" Anula whispered.

"Yes," I said. But I wasn't sure at all.

I slumped to test the rope and cloth that bound us. It held tight and I allowed my tired body to relax in the makeshift tree bed. My eyelids wavered and slowly closed. I thought of nothing but what I could hear and feel: my heartbeat, thudding in my chest, the warm summer air tickling my sweaty skin… and the monkeys, screeching…

"Anula!" I sat up. "Why is it so noisy?"

"Shhh, I'm trying to sleep," she muttered. "It's nothing, we're in the forest, of course there's going to be noises…"

As the words left her mouth a noble roar echoed through the rainforest and everything stopped. Nothing dared move or make the smallest of sounds. Even the trees and plants around me seemed to have halted every tiny movement, from the quietest fall of a leaf or sway of a branch. I imagined Limpy's round eyes darting around, searching, but he too was still.

For a few moments, the forest was under a dark spell – was I the only one breathing in this eerie darkness? Tiny goose bumps prickled on my skin.

A tiger was out there. Somewhere nearby. We were in its home. That made us its food.

"That roar," Anula whispered. "The tiger must have just eaten, and tigers only eat every three days."

I relaxed a little. "That's good," I said.

"Unless we come across a different tiger…" Anula's voice trailed off. I shivered.

"Are you scared, Leeta?"

"No. Are you?"

"No."

"Good."

I closed my eyes. I took three deep, slow belly breaths and tried to relax. "Anula?"

"Yeah?"

"I am scared," I breathed. "I'm so scared. I wish I was home."

"Me too," Anula answered in a small voice. "Well, we could head back..."

I smiled. She reminded me of Seera sometimes. "Goodnight Anula."

Chapter 10: Training

Patish

Like the bellow of an angry bull, the roar of a conch plucked me out of the depths of the darkness where I had escaped to for the night. Recollecting where I was, I opened my eyes to see a flap of our shelter open.

A loud commanding voice followed. "Get up! Get up and line up!"

My legs were stiff from yesterday's long march down the Valley and memories of the day's events began to return to my head. Still sleepy, I turned over to ponder things as I like to do before rising, but this was no ordinary day in Shaktin. The murmurs and footsteps of the other boys moving quickly out of the tent reminded me of Discipline. I forced myself up to join them.

Outside, the pre-dawn air was fresh and still. I followed the others to a clearing where boys were lining up. How they knew what to do was beyond me. As I scrambled and searched for a place to stand, a hand grabbed my arm and pulled me into a line.

"Quick Patish, before the final conch is blown. What happened to you last night? I thought we'd lost you."

It was Laksa, my new friend.

Before I could answer, another conch bellowed out demanding our instant attention. Total stillness followed until a commanding voice broke the silence. It came from a shadowy form at the front of our lines. A few stragglers slipped into the lines quietly to avoid being noticed.

"Salutations." The commander joined the palms of his hands in front of his chest and slightly bowed his head.

Instinctively I joined in the response, for I knew it well – Diipundi would always commence our training sessions in the same way.

"Salutations, Commander." A thousand voices spoke and gestured as one.

The commander spoke. "For those of you who arrived yesterday, every morning you will rise before sunrise with the call of the conch and line up here. The Salutations and other postures which you are about to learn will give you discipline of the mind. You have all heard our great Master Vinyak say that, for an army, discipline is the secret of success. That discipline begins in the mind of each and every one of its soldiers. With this, you will learn to control your breathing, and with the control of your breath, you will learn to control every muscle and every movement of your body. Only then can you conquer fear in the face of battle."

Diipundi too had talked of this: "Control your breathing, and you will calm your mind; calm your mind and you will see more clearly in times of confusion. When your instincts and emotions are confusing your judgement, calm your breathing and you will calm your mind." I wondered what Diipundi would think of the Salutations as preparation for war!

The commander took a few steps forward and continued. "Now, every second person, take one step forward."

Laksa took a step forward, so I stood still.

"The first Salutation is to the Ancestors. Feet together, now breathe in slowly... one, two, three... now breathing out even more slowly, out one, out two, and out three, now in again as you raise your arms high..."

I went through the motions automatically, at times taking care not to get ahead of the commander who guided us step by step. Amazing. They were identical to the ones I'd learnt and practised so often with Leeta and Seera under the guidance of Diipundi. Silently, I completed the Salutations to the Ancestors in all four directions.

"Once more, a Salutation to the Rising Sun," the Commander said, as the sky awakened.

I could tell it was going to be another hot day. Birds in the trees called busily and a distant rooster crowed repeatedly. No one spoke as the commander walked around inspecting us, correcting any sloppy postures.

As we sat on the ground ready for our next instructions, I turned to Laksa. "Thanks for pulling me into the line, I didn't know what was going on."

Janam and Talbik were sitting next to Laksa and lent forward as I spoke.

"Last night," I started, "I got lost in the darkness and wandered down to the river. You won't believe this, but the Pauravans were singing our song."

"Yeah, often happens in villages across the river. Sort of becomes a competition to see who can sing best," said Janam, stopping abruptly to listen to the commander.

"Next, we do the Postures of Animals which will give you the special qualities of the animal. First the Cobra, which can strike a mortal blow quick as lightning!"

The commander motioned with his hand poised like a cobra and flung it forward for an imaginary bite. He demonstrated by lying face down on the ground like a snake. Again, I thought of Diipundi, who had taught us the same posture for flexibility.

It was our turn, and we all lay face down. My hands flat on the earth, I slowly raised my head and arched my torso until I was looking almost straight up into the sky.

"Hold this posture to the count of eight," the commander ordered, counting aloud to eight. "Now repeat it eight times," and we did.

In the upward and downward movements of this posture, my eyes had been flicking around to see if I could spot anyone from Shaktin. In a row to my left, I spotted Tomay, but he was looking forward and didn't see me.

"The Peacock," the commander went on, "is a more difficult posture which develops balance and strength, especially the strength of wrists. When you thrust a lance, the strength of your grip is paramount. Come here boy!" He pointed into the lines and a young conscript jumped up. It was Liddu.

"Here, take this." He gave Liddu a long bamboo lance he'd picked up from the ground. "Now thrust it hard at me as if I were an enemy about to kill you!"

Liddu didn't hesitate, and for a moment, I thought he was going to stab the commander, but in a single motion, the commander parried it away with the outside of his wrist, grabbed it and swung it around, hitting Liddu on the arm with enough force to knock him down.

Liddu looked up wide-eyed and we let out a collective gasp as the commander stood over him ready to plunge the lance into him.

"Then of course you finish him," and he thrust the lance into the ground close to Liddu's stomach.

"You," he said to Liddu, who was pale with shock, "what's your name?"

"Liddu, sir," he answered, his voice quivering.

"Get your things ready, you're going to the Messenger tent. You're too young to fight. You'll only create a weakness in our wall. Can you run?"

Liddu nodded, disappointment on his face.

"Then you'll make a good messenger," he said, turning to us. "Now watch," he commanded, knowing he had our undivided attention. "Start by squatting, then knees apart, hands flat on the ground pointing backwards to your feet, then slowly move your body forward, rest your weight onto your elbows, and support the body in a horizontal position… and hold it."

His body was straight and balanced parallel to the ground, with all his weight on his elbows. The resemblance to a peacock was obvious. The bulging ripples in his arms and legs showed the strain involved in maintaining the rigid balance of this posture. I squatted to execute it and looked around to see how the others would go. It looked easy enough when he did it, but few managed to hold it for more than a few moments before toppling over.

The commander brought his knees forward, touched his feet to the ground and rose. "Your minds are all over the place, not in control of your bodies! You have little time to learn this difficult art, but you will learn nothing until you empty your minds of those heroic deeds you thought you were coming here to achieve as simply as picking a mango from a tree. In a matter of days when the moon is full, you will engage a fierce enemy who wants to live and conquer just as much as you do. And when you meet in battle and stare into his eyes, you will see that he is intent on killing you before you can kill him. That is the moment when discipline and control of your body will count. I've seen strong, fully-grown men go weak at the knees when the real fighting begins. Now take control, control your breathing, control your mind, and control your body."

We tried it again and went through more postures: the Lion, for bravery; the Rhino, for strength; the Monkey for agility; and finally, the Crane, a posture I knew well, for concentration and determination.

As usual, the commander spoke as he demonstrated. "Breathe in… now lift one foot up… bring your heel up against the thigh… steady… raising your arms up high, hands together like a head of an arrow… keep them up high, hold still, now breathe slowly and concentrate your gaze on something in front of you." He looked straight as an arrow himself, and he stared intensely like he was burning a hole into his enemy with his eyes. "Keeping your gaze fixed, as you breathe in, lift your heel slowly so you are standing on your toes, and hold this pose for as long as you can, as if your life depended on it!"

With the ease that comes from practise, I completed the arrow, raised the heel of my left foot, and balanced on my toes.

Around me, the sounds of feet hitting the dirt were followed by grumbles of frustration as I fixed my concentration on an orange flag above a tent. Once I had fixed my stare, it was like an invisible force holding me up, keeping me steady, balanced.

"Life is about balance," Diipundi would say, and Satu and I would compete out in the fields to see who could balance the longest. Of course, we knew what he really meant: balancing things in life, like opposite emotions, having fun and being serious, experiencing fear but being courageous.

More sounds of feet hit the dirt, and soon the attention was all on the few boys who remained. The competition was on. I knew that Satu would be one still upright, and though I couldn't turn to see where he was, I could feel the competition between us, just like in the fields of Shaktin.

The trainer continued to walk around. "Only four left up!" he commented, "Everyone else squat down."

I felt the stares of hundreds of eyes on me and almost lost my balance, but I took a calming breath and steadied, fixing my sight back onto the orange flag. In the total silence, a soft thud and the murmurs of congratulatory voices told me only three were left. I stared harder as the muscles in my raised arms and my left leg were straining. My toes and the ball of my foot were supporting my whole weight, but the real contest now was between my own muscles and my mind, competing not to give in first. Soon another thud and excited voices told me that it was now a contest between two; I just knew that the other was Satu, out there, still upright, and balanced.

The commander walked up in front of me and looked me up and down, checking to see that I hadn't relaxed my posture.

"Good, now fight beyond what you think you are capable of. When you think you're done, fight the pain and go on for another moment, and then another, and take a breath, ignore the pain, and hold!"

I had already reached the point where every moment was a struggle, my bent toes yearning to relax, my raised arms pleading to drop. My body implored me to stop, but I stared even harder at the flag and took slow purposeful breaths. The intensity of every feeling was channelled into a battle between my sheer willpower and my mercy-seeking senses. I knew I couldn't go on much longer, but, each time I wanted to give in, I fought it for just an instant, then another instant, clutching at thoughts of Mother, Leeta, Seera, and Father.

For you, I thought in another instant. The memory of Seera helplessly looking at me when I put her down after our last hug... the swelling tears in her eyes... beads of sweat from my armpits rolled down the sides of my rib cage.

Another instant passed, then my concentration burst like a bubble. With a thud my foot involuntarily flattened on the earth and my arms dropped automatically to swing freely with relief. In that very instant after my own foot touched the ground, I heard another thud from a distance. Trainees jumped up to cheer and congratulate the champions of the moment. Laksa, Janam and Talbik proudly embraced me amongst the small crowd of well-wishers.

"Hey, you're a legend now, Patish!" Talbik shouted jokingly for all to hear. I couldn't help grinning, embarrassed though I was at the attention this minor feat was bringing. I looked at my new friends and smiled.

A little crowd had gathered around the other final competitor. Amongst them were Tomay, Sujas, Asten and Liddu standing around Satu, who looked up and saw me approaching. The others saw me, too, giving congratulations and hugs as if I'd won some major event like the Valley Sprint.

"Hey, Patish, equal champion!"

"Shaktin rules."

"Our Patish and Satu drew."

"Well done, Patish, we tied again." Satu said, referring to the numerous times we'd both hung on, facing each other, and giving up in the same exasperated moment.

"No, you won it, Satu, you're the champion today," I said, knowing that the sound of Satu's foot landing clearly followed my own, even if only by an instant. I put my arm around his shoulder to hug him as I did so often before, then we looked into each other's eyes to see who was really there. Was it the best friend we had grown up with, or was it another, a changed person, an unrecognisable character inside the guise of that lifelong friend?

Satu avoided that question, but asked another: "Patish, the Rolpur boy Vinto is in a bad way, can you help?"

I looked at him, trying to hide my disappointment that there was no acknowledgement of me, no asking how I was, where I had spent the night, who I was with... like what we'd have talked about if things were back to normal.

"Well, it was quite a whipping," I said.

"He became delirious last night and couldn't wake up this morning. He's got a fever and has been covered in sweat. He's like that boy Ratul at the Valley Games. Have you got any of that healing balm from Diipundi?"

"I didn't bring it," I said, "It's not like I had time to pack thoroughly!"

I appealed silently to the others, expecting some understanding and support, but instead I saw something in the way they gaped at me, something that made me uncomfortable. Had Satu told them about our falling out?

"Of course, I'd get it if I had it, but I don't!" I declared. My best friends, my very own village brothers, seemed like they couldn't believe their ears. Lost for words, I looked away.

***

A breakfast of cracked wheat gruel with salt gave Talbik, Laksa and Janam plenty to joke about as we sat outside our tent. I couldn't help being quiet, reflecting on my words with Satu and the others.

"I don't know who was on mess duty for breakfast, but they did a good job of making a mess!" Janam quipped in his jovial style, arousing a bit of laughter.

"Well, it was mess duty after all," said Laksa, not wanting to miss out on the joking.

"Yes, and at least we know why Commander Rixten eats alone," teased Talbik, "so he doesn't have to eat that slop. Did anyone see what he was having?"

Janam and Laksa looked at Talbik and waited, knowing they were about to find out.

"I saw him feasting on mango and bananas," said Talbik. "With fresh curd, and pancakes fried in butter. He has his own cook!"

"Don't let the soldiers hear you, or you'll be having a taste of Discipline for lunch!" warned Laksa, half serious as a couple of soldiers walked past nearby.

When they were out of listening range, Talbik turned to me with a glimmer of an idea in his eye. "Patish, do you know when the supplies from your village will arrive? You could get some decent food before it's all turned over to the commanders. What do you say?"

"Good idea, but I haven't got a clue about it," I answered. "I'm not even sure that food will be brought."

"Every village must send a cart full of food to help feed the army. Ours has already been, but you only arrived last night, so yours will probably arrive in a few days. You can see them coming over there, near that bunch of trees."

I wondered, if a cart of food was sent from Shaktin, perhaps Diipundi would include some healing balm, and even if he didn't, I could ask the driver to get him to send some. It was worth a try.

After breakfast, it was time to put on our uniforms for weapons training.

I took my cloth, unfolded it, and wrapped it over my shoulders and across my chest before tying the ends behind my back.

I felt a sense of pride thinking that this was the same uniform that my own father had worn. I had played at being a soldier countless times with Satu and our friends, imagining the glory of this very moment, the chance to be a hero for our country. It was the game we all loved most. We played lots of versions; using sticks as swords, long pieces of bamboo as spears, and hand to hand combat, wrestling any time the opportunity arose.

It hadn't always been so. When I was younger, I never joined in these games as Mother had raised us to believe that we should never hurt a living creature. It was only after I had been pushed over and kicked repeatedly by a group of boys at a Valley Festival about five years ago that Mother took Leeta and me to Diipundi to ask him to train us in the defensive arts of which he was a Master. The Way of Peace he called it; mystical ways learnt from the Purple Sage. A way of thinking, or "being" as Diipundi would say.

The moves he taught us for defending ourselves always amazed me, and they proved surprisingly effective whenever I used them in play. But, like Mother, Diipundi always spoke of it as a way of minimising hurt to any sentient creature. "Live in such a way that you treat every person as a friend," he would say. "But if someone is aggressive, remember the Three Tiers of Noble Action from the Purple Sage. Face aggression with kindness. If that fails, flee to safety, but if that fails, use every means possible to defend yourself."

I couldn't help being troubled by the fact that, even though Paurava was threatening to attack us, it was our own prince inviting this war by the building of the canal. Had there been talks to find a compromise? I didn't know and would never know.

The collection of conscripted boys now looked like a battalion of young soldiers standing in lines of ten, red uniforms on and ready for orders. Waiting in the early morning sun, I noticed Asten two rows up, and, to my left, in the third row from the front, was Satu. I counted only nine in his row and thought of Vinto who was struggling to recover from the whipping. I pondered what Satu's reaction would be when I told him I hadn't brought the healing balm. I suppose it was understandable, because "Little Diipundi" had become my nickname anytime anyone grazed a knee or spilled a drop of blood from a cut. I had always played the healer and my little ceramic container of beeswax and sage was never far away.

The waiting continued and our straight lines disintegrated into groups of boys exchanging stories. Talbik was arguing about the weapons we would be given when everyone stood up straight and faced the front.

Coming from the commander's tent were Master Vinyak and Commander Rixten. Four soldiers followed behind, each carrying a long pole with a narrow flag half its length. The flags were made of red cloth, probably the same as the uniforms we wore, but each had different markings.

Commander Rixten addressed us. "Soldiers of the youth battalion, salutations. I am proud to look at you in the uniform of the Army of Gandhara, ready to defend your country, your people, and your prince."

He spoke with much greater confidence than yesterday. He gave Master Vinyak a slight look, a novice glancing to the master for approval. After yesterday's debacle, Master Vinyak was probably here to make sure that everything was done properly. After all, our survival would depend on how well we were trained.

"For those of you who arrived yesterday," he said, "this is the formation for your daily battle training. You are in your four units. Look at your flag and memorise it so you know it the moment you see it."

The four soldiers with flags had taken a position in front of each column, their flags straight, tall and visible. The red flag at the front of my line had a yellow circle, and inside it a blue shape of an eagle's head. The other three flags had the same yellow circle, but each flag had a different animal's head in the circle. There was a rhino, a cobra, and a tiger.

"In battle," said Commander Rixten, "you may not be able to hear commands, you may not know what to do, which way to go. Your flag will become your commander.

"When you see it raised, like that," he said, pointing to the flagbearers who lifted their flagpoles into little pouches strapped around their chests, "you will be poised to spring into action. And when it is lent forward…" He raised his arm straight up as if it were a flag then tilted it forward, mimicked by the flagbearers. "…then you will strike." He pretended to thrust a lance into an imaginary enemy.

He so reminded me of the games we played, killing imaginary enemies with the greatest of ease. Commander Rixten was probably young enough to have played with us. I wondered if he had ever fought in a real battle.

"Today," he said, "we are honoured to have Master Vinyak here to begin your training in the art of Kalari, the Way of the Battlefield."

The Master stood perfectly straight, his every gaze and movement precise. He seemed hardly human, his very presence commanding respect. Perhaps he was some sort of a god, a God of War, I mused.

"Soldiers of the yellow circle," Master Vinyak said, eyes connecting with each and every one of us. "Your weapon is the bamboo lance, the simplest, but most versatile of weapons." As he spoke, he stretched his arm forward, holding up a long, straight, bamboo lance with a pointed metal head. "Learn to respect your weapon, hold it as often as you can with each of your hands until it feels like an extension of your own body so that without looking, you know exactly where its spearhead is." He took three steps forward, the bamboo in his hand remaining upright, almost dancing when he moved.

"I salute the ancestors," Master Vinyak's voice was humble as he kneeled and bowed to touch the earth with his forehead, "and the Earth Goddess."

I was surprised to hear his dedication to the Earth Goddess, expecting a dedication to the God of Fire.

He stood up slowly, with the bamboo cane held in both hands. With an explosion of energy, he began swinging the cane, twirling it, thrusting, parrying, and blocking blows from imaginary enemies. He used both ends in forward and backward thrusts, then swung the pointed end through the air with such force that it would have sliced off the heads of a dozen soldiers. A twirl in his hands and the cane thrust forward and back, up high overhead then across an arc in slashes that would surely have seen another dozen enemies fall down dead. A backward kick fended off an imaginary attacker as the cane swung around to finish him off, then another series of twirls, thrusts and slashes even more vigorous than before, and in multiple directions would surely have stopped half an army in its tracks.

I imagined the scene, the surviving attackers fleeing for their lives before the deadly cane started swinging again.

The demonstration over, Master Vinyak drew his feet together and, in a salute to his weapon, held it in front of him and bowed his head.

***

Raise the cane, I recalled, bring it down and thrust, swing the end around upwards to stun, then turn the point around and plunge to finish off the enemy. Not that our canes had a real spearhead, nor was there an enemy. Again, and again and again, we went through the routine: raise the cane, bring it down and thrust, swing the end upwards to stun, then turn the point around and plunge it in to finish off the enemy.

Into the air we thrust and blocked until the sun was high, our throats parched, and our aching limbs covered in sweat.

Finally, a halt to the drills was called, and we headed back to our tents for shade, food, and rest. I was too exhausted even to speak.

Talbik wasn't. "I hope the enemy behave exactly like that, because that's all my body can do now, I don't think I could move in any other way!"

"Yes," added Laksa, "and I hope we get spearheads before the Pauravans attack!"

Chapter 11: Assassins

Leeta

There was no denying it. Since that almighty roar of the tiger last night, we were scared. Real scared. Scared to the bone.

The forest seemed so serene when we first entered. Now it was anything but. Anywhere I looked it was much the same – a maze of trees, bushes, and creepers, with no path to follow, and no idea what was slinking in the shadows.

"Earthmother, guidance is needed," I thought, closing my eyes.

Three things came to me. The first was that we were going uphill, so at least we could be sure we weren't going around in circles. Every step was a step closer to the Abode of the Purple Sage, which meant we were almost there. I couldn't let fear stop me now.

Secondly, I came to realise that hidden friends surrounded us. The continual noises of the forest were actually comforting. I knew that if I could hear the sweet whistles of birds, the choruses of cicadas and the idle chatter of monkeys, there was no tiger lurking.

And then there was the final reason I was able to calm my forest-jitters. He was walking so close that occasionally I felt the warmth of his breath on my calves: Limpy. With him strolling happily behind me, it was like another day in Shaktin.

In front of us, Anula halted. "Finally, water," she said, heading toward a clearing. She had barely shown the hint of a smile so far this morning. Maybe it was all getting to her, too.

"Thank you, Earthmother, for providing for us," I murmured.

"It's just water and this *is* a rainforest," Anula replied. She crouched down to the trickling stream and cupped her fingers.

I wasn't far behind her. And nor was Limpy, who gulped and slurped until his thirst was quenched.

When I'd had enough, I untied my pack and took the opportunity to fill my water gourd. I put it back with my other things onto the cloth, but as I tied it, I realised something was wrong. It couldn't be... I was missing the most important thing of all. The Wisdom Wheel, wrapped in the map – where was it?

"Anula..." my voice squeaked. "The Wisdom Wheel isn't here."

Facing away from me in the stream, Anula stopped. "What?"

"The Wisdom Wheel and the map, they're not here." I could feel my cheeks turning red. This wasn't right. I was trying to think back. Had I picked them up after our sleep? Surely, I wouldn't have forgotten them.

I spotted Anula's bag on the ground and reached for it. "You don't have it, do you?"

"Hey!" Anula cried out. "You had the map! Why would it be in there?"

"I don't know, but we have to check!" I tipped her bag upside down. Her pointy edged comb, knife, water container and remaining bread fell into the dirt. I quickly rescued the food and blew the dust away.

"There," said Anula. "Happy now? You've ruined my lunch!"

"I don't get it," I said, pulling my fingers through my hair. "I did *not* lose them, I didn't..."

Anula stood up. "Well clearly you did!" She spat the words. "I can't believe this! I can't!"

I shook my head. My mind raced between the events of going to sleep last night in the tree and our walking this morning. I looked through the contents of the bag once more.

Anula's face was bright red. "It's over," she said softly. "Our mission is over."

"It's not," I said. But I was thinking that, too.

"It is! We need that Wisdom Wheel to give to the Mountain People!"

I stared at the ground. We would be lost without the map and Wisdom Wheel – that's what Diipundi had said. The Mountain People wouldn't help us without the Wheel.

"We'll go back," I said, facing Anula.

"It's our only option now," she agreed. "Your mother will understand."

"No!" I said, "I mean we'll go back and look for it. We'll retrace our steps."

Anula shook her head. "Leeta, we're in the middle of the forest. How would we find anything here?"

"We can't just give up!"

"Well, if we don't find the map," Anula crossed her arms, "the only thing we can do is return to Shaktin. The Mountain People protect the Sage, and the Wheel is the only right to passage they'll recognise."

"We'll think of something," I said.

Anula's eyes bulged. "*You'll* think of something? Here we go again, Leeta trying to be the hero. Is this about your brother? Are you still trying to prove yourself against him?" Anula's words flew at me like arrows.

"What! No!" I spluttered. "How dare you!"

"It's true. Everyone knows it." Anula's black eyes were unrelenting.

"Shut up," I said, knowing we couldn't afford to waste time on this argument, "and help me look for the Wheel."

I took several paces back downhill, peering carefully into the bushes. I gazed at rocks and dirt and green plants. It was ridiculous. There was as much chance of the monsoon starting as there was of finding the Wheel now.

"We're never going to find it," Anula said. "If we go back to Shaktin and talk to Diipundi…"

As she spoke, I noticed that Limpy's attention had been caught by something. He was tense, ears pointed forward, tail down. He began a small guttural growl.

"Anula! Stop!" I whispered, pointing to Limpy.

"So?"

"Shhh," I commanded. "I can hear something."

We listened. It sounded like plopping. Like someone was relieving themselves. Anula scrunched her face; we were thinking the same thing.

"Is that a boar with diarrhoea?" she joked.

"Shhh!" I whispered again, wanting to laugh but realising the danger of making a sound. "Whatever it was came from over there…"

Anula's hand smothered my mouth. She pointed a little to the right where I could just make out the shape of a man rising.

I gestured to an area further away from the man. Anula nodded. We moved slowly, carefully finding a quiet landing for every step.

Then we heard voices. Barely audible but distinct. I grabbed Limpy, stroking his head to stop him from barking.

Anula motioned silently, pointing to herself and then towards the voices. She cupped her hand around her ear to hear what they were saying. She started creeping towards them. I kept stroking Limpy and followed. Could the voices belong to the Mountain People? I didn't think we were high enough to have reached them already.

We heard some crunching footsteps, and then voices and figures became clear. Three men were sitting on fallen trees in a gully below us, and beyond them was a whole camp of men. They were speaking our tongue. *Soldiers.* I could only just distinguish their blue-grey uniform, worn by all except two of the three sitting closer to us. They wore the same deep red uniforms as the soldiers who had taken Patish.

I took a few quick steps to the side, desperate to be hidden behind the nearby tree. Anula had stopped behind an outcropping freckled white rock and lay on it, peering above it to see. Oblivious to our concerns, Limpy continued to enjoy the affection I was giving him and lifted his head back to be stroked under the jaw.

"You must not fire until the battle begins," one of the solders said. "It must look like part of the battle!"

The man wearing red was drawing on the ground with a pointy stick. "See, the prince's platform will be here, backed up against the Boulders of Dharma, a large rock big as a temple with a smaller rock sitting on top of it. You cannot miss it – it stands out alone on the flood plain of the river. Your archers will be here, hidden behind the boulders. From there you can strike your fatal blow." His voice was strong, but he spoke matter-of-factly. *Orders are orders.*

"But how will we know when the battle starts?" said the soldier in blue. "We'll be behind the rocks so we can't be seen."

"When the drumming stops and the trumpets are blown to attack, the battle flag will be raised by the Royal Guard. Have a lookout watching and wait a few moments before you let loose your arrows at the flag. The prince and his guards will be killed. Keep your horses ready and ride off as quickly as possible. You must not risk capture. No one must find out where you are from."

I was totally absorbed in this when a soft kick in the chest from Limpy's flaying leg brought my attention back to him. He was wriggling hard, trying to free himself from my arms. I believed I could calm him with a severe look, but his attention was elsewhere. Then I saw, just above us on a thick branch, a cobra, its shiny black scales glistening in the few rays of sunlight. I took an instinctive step backward, snapping the dry stem of a dead bush behind me.

"What was that?" a soldier spoke.

I froze behind the tree.

"Probably just a wild fowl," said another.

My heart was racing.

The cobra did not move, but I could see its small black eyes fixed on me. With a slight hiss, the reptile opened a wide hood below its head, threatening. Limpy whimpered and I rushed to muzzle his mouth with my hands. Too late.

"*That* was more than a bird," said the first voice again.

"Could be the sound of lunch," said the other. "Show us your marksmanship!"

Leaves crunched, and I knew a soldier was coming toward me. I edged sideways, keeping the tree trunk between me and the approaching archer like the game of hide and seek I played with Seera and Patish as a child. But this was no game.

Anula's face was pale with fright. She pointed with her finger, twice, desperately trying to communicate something to me. I shook my head at first, then I realised exactly what she meant. The archer was almost in line with the rock she was hiding behind. If he passed it, she would be in view.

I had to distract the soldier. I lowered Limpy onto the ground. Once they saw that the noise had come from a cute little three-legged dog, the soldiers would back off. My arms were shaking. I pushed Limpy forwards from behind the tree.

Thwack!

A tensioned bowstring sprang, propelling an arrow through the air and through Limpy's neck. His body thumped against the ground, flung sideways from the lethal force of the arrow. I threw my hands over my mouth to stop myself from screaming. One sound and the next arrow would be through my own heart.

"Ha, it's only got three legs!" cried a voice. There was no remorse; he sounded gleeful.

"Dirty little scavenger," said the other. "I'm not eating that dog for lunch."

"Mangy old thing."

His footsteps told me he was receding. Anula was still crouched behind the boulder. Her eyes were glassy.

Eventually, I heard the soldiers' jovial voices heading back to their camp. I lowered myself down against the tree trunk and pulled my legs up to my chest. The snake – I remembered it with a jolt and twisted my head to look up at the branch. It was gone. I wondered if I'd imagined it being there in the first place. My fingertips tingled. I was numb all over.

I sat in silence, waiting. After awhile I heard distant noise from the archers' camp. I stood up and peered out from behind the tree. They had packed their camp and were leaving.

Anula was still sitting behind the boulder, body tucked into a tight little ball, head down.

Limpy's lifeless body lay in the grass, the arrow protruding from his neck. Blowflies buzzed at the pool of blood that had drained away his life.

I edged closer to him on my hands and knees. His brown eyes were still open, pink tongue hanging out the side of his mouth. But the mischievous, spirited dog, my dearest little friend, was gone.

Anula crawled over to us. Tears dripped down from her chin and onto his cold body as she closed his eyes with two fingers.

Carefully, I broke the arrowhead and pulled the arrow out from Limpy's flesh.

We covered his body with grass and leaves, concealing the wound and his tail, and the ears he'd so loved being stroked, until all that was left was the front of his little head.

"My little one," I murmured as I softly dropped leaves over his face.

Anula took my hand and squeezed. I squeezed back, and she embraced me.

"Leeta?" Anula whispered.

I couldn't stop staring at Limpy's innocent little body covered in leaves, no longer full of energy and life. He'd trusted me. I did this to him.

"It's not your fault, Leeta."

I wiped my eyes with the back of my hand. "I pushed him." My voice shook. "I pushed him. And I insisted he come with us. You were right."

"You didn't shoot that arrow," Anula said. "You didn't kill him, Leeta."

I sobbed. "Why did they do this? He was just a dog. He was the best dog. I can't believe this. I can't."

Anula had no answer. "Look, we need to find shelter before it becomes too dark," she said.

Two entire kingdoms were preparing for war, and now we knew that trained assassins were on a mission to kill the prince himself. And yet here we were, two defenceless Shaktin girls somewhere in the middle of a rainforest. I corrected myself: two hopeless Shaktin girls who had lost the Wisdom Wheel, the map, and a three-legged dog.

"Maybe you were right, Anula. Maybe we have to go back." But as the words left my lips, I thought of Mother's solemn face if we were to return to Shaktin now. She would pretend to be proud, I imagined. She would kiss me on the cheek, purse her lips and smile in the same way she used to smile when we lost Father. Mouth stretched out, teeth showing, even dimples in her cheeks. Her eyes, of course, would be heavy with the pain she tried to hide. They never deceived.

"No!" Anula cried as if there was another threat nearby, but there was none. She gulped. "I mean, *no*; we can't give up like this."

I sighed. "Can't we?"

"You're so glum!" she said.

"Reminds you of someone, does it?"

"I don't know who you're talking about." she said with a hint of playfulness in her voice. "Come on, Leeta. Don't be so selfish. Just be the hero for a little while more. Please?" When I didn't answer, she tugged on my arm. "Limpy would not be impressed if you just stayed here forever."

I wasn't sure what I wanted anymore.

Chapter 12: Manhood

Patish

In a strange sort of way, I actually felt settled, almost enjoying the training. Every day seemed to have a pattern: the salutation postures before sunrise, breakfast, then battle drills until we dropped with exhaustion in the heat of midday. Lunch was followed by a welcome afternoon nap, when it was too hot to do anything else anyway.

I lay down in the shade of our tent, its sides rolled up to allow us the fresh air of a breeze in case there was one, which there wasn't. When I woke up from the afternoon nap, everyone from our tent had already gone. I had been in a deep sleep, dreaming I was at the well in Shaktin, and Satu had been spilling the water from the bucket every time I went to fill my clay pot for Mother. He kept laughing and teasing how I was letting Mother down, and my anger had kept growing and growing into a deeper and deeper frustration. The dream and the frustration faded from my mind, and I picked up a jug of water for a drink.

Cries of "Kabbadi, Kabbadi!" with the laughter of a crowd told me what everyone was doing. The game of Kabbadi was a favourite pastime amongst the soldiers, and in the afternoons many a game could be found being contested around the camp. At the Valley Festival, it was the most prestigious event for village teams to win, and, with the strongest men of the village filling the team, it was almost impossible for boys our age to play. So here, the boys were relishing the opportunity to play against each other and the strongest were gaining reputations quickly.

The excitement was already high, and a "battle" was raging on the field. I spotted Laksa in the role of the raider as he burst into a sprint, chasing down and tagging three opposition players while yelling "Kabaddi, Kabaddi, Kabaddi..." He turned and ran for his life, still yelling as a couple of opposition stoppers closed in on him.

A huge boy from training swung his arms to clasp Laksa around the chest, but before he could secure the hold, Laksa cleverly dropped to the ground and scampered out of reach, still muttering "Kabaddi" as he found his feet. Another two stoppers chased desperately, trying to catch him before he made it back to the safety of his team's home line. One of them just managed to grab Laksa and cling to him as he propelled himself and the clinging stopper over the line.

Cheers broke out all around the ground, and I clapped enthusiastically along with everyone for Laksa's bravery and speed. My hands were still clapping when my eyes met those of the failed stopper as he picked himself up from the dust. It was Satu.

A conch roared not far from where Satu and I stood. I wanted to say something, to explain that I didn't know that it was him, and that Laksa was a new friend... but there was no time; a conch demanded immediate attention.

Commander Rixten stood between two flag bearers to address us. "Soldiers of the Youth Brigade, I have an important announcement." With each address, he grew more confident, perhaps because we paid greater attention.

"You all know that the greatest service you can perform, the greatest sacrifice you can make, is to put your lives on the battlefield to protect your families, your country, and your prince. To perform this service, to make this sacrifice, is a privilege that the Gods have given to men. As you are under the age of fifteen and have yet to have your Manhood Ritual, we will reward your willingness to volunteer in the army of Gandhara by giving you a special collective Manhood Ritual ceremony."

We hadn't volunteered at all. I imagined raising my arm and asking, "Sir, if we didn't volunteer, if we were forced to come against the will of our Elders, are we then free to go?" But I said nothing. There was no free speech here, only Discipline.

"Tomorrow you will fast," continued the commander, "from sunrise to the sunrise of the next day, the Fourth Day of the Dark Lunar Fortnight. It is an auspicious day for your Manhood Ritual Ceremony. As the moon grows strong and begins to dominate the sky, so too you will begin as men to realise your destiny."

After the evening meal, where we had all eaten as much as we possibly could in preparation for the fast, I told Laksa and the others that I wasn't feeling well and so I wasn't going to attend the night's entertainment with them. I went into our tent and lay down to rest, waiting until their voices were gone.

In the darkness, I made my way over to where Satu's tent was. I could make out shapes with the distant light from flaming torches. Not knowing if Satu was amongst them, I whistled the tune that Martal had taught us. With the background noises of everyone settling in before the flame dancers started, I whistled louder a few times until I saw a shape heading towards me while the others left for the entertainment. It was Satu.

"Patish, I knew it would be you," he said. "What's happened...? When I saw you cheering against me in Kabbadi..." He dropped his gaze for a moment then looked up straight at me. "I knew I had to confront you. Why have you turned on me so?"

"Satu, you've always been like a brother..."

"Patish, I've always regarded you *as* a brother. Maybe that's where we differ."

"No, that's not what I mean. I too..."

"Then how could you have even thought of joining that liar Rakti? And you just ignored my plea for help with healing balm for the Rolpur boy. They've been picking on me at every chance, saying I lied about getting help for their friend."

"But I've been watching for our supply cart, hoping Diipundi may have sent me a pot of balm," I explained.

"Then where were you this afternoon when it arrived before the Kabbadi?"

"Satu, I'm sorry, I was sleeping. I didn't even know it had come! And I didn't even know you were in the game. I was just cheering for Laksa, a new friend I've made."

Satu looked away and went quiet. I couldn't believe the difficulty I was having trying to explain what had happened. The words just weren't carrying the message from my heart. As soon as I'd said: "new friend", I could see he felt betrayed. Again. Whatever I said, things just seemed to keep getting worse.

"Did you hear the commander talk about volunteering?" I asked. "And the Manhood ritual? I'm going to ask him for a Shaktin ritual."

"Patish, are you crazy? You will just attract the wrong sort of attention. You know how some scorn us – what if the commander is like that? I know what this is really about – you're just too scared to fight and this is another of your schemes, like the one with Rakti!"

I pushed Satu in the chest with open hands, almost knocking him over. He regained his balance, glaring at me, before leaving without another word. I stood in shock and disbelief. What had I done?

***

The next day after our drills, I went to see Commander Rixten.

"As you wish," he said to my request. He even summoned Martal to instruct me in the Shaktin manhood initiation. That was a while ago, before nightfall. I stopped thinking about it and looked back along the riverbed towards the camp.

No longer could I see a single campfire or torch. In every direction, there was only darkness. I listened to the night sounds of earth buzzing with life. The calls of nearby frogs stopped as I approached.

This fulfilled the first of Martal's instructions: "Find a place where you are totally alone, away from any other person."

Using a cane staff, I was ready to fulfil the second instruction: "Mark a spot in the earth. It will be your sacred spot. Before sitting on it, remove your clothing, and any objects you might have, even your necklace, which I recognise as your father's. Take with you this thread five times the length of your forearm."

Even in the darkness, the light colour of the sand was easy to see, and I sidestepped, marking a spot. I untied my cloth and let it fall to the ground. Carefully, I removed my necklace and held it for a moment, thinking of how Father must have gone through this ritual himself. I remembered Mother's words the day she had tied it around my neck.

"This was your father's. Wear it with honour and always remember how much he loved you." Mother's words stayed true, for I always have.

I could never forget Father. Even seven years after he was killed, I could still feel the strength of his grip as he held me by the hands, swinging me up high like a bird in the sky, then down low with my feet skimming across the top of the wild grasses, like a crane about to land. His white teeth shone through a bursting grin as he watched me in blissful flight, my eyes fixed on him in adoration. Then with one powerful manoeuvre, he would swing me up high so I landed on his shoulders, squealing with delight as my arms clung around his neck. We'd laugh and I knew I was sitting on the bravest, strongest man in the world. In Father's presence, I knew no fear or worry. I remembered that happiness... full, free, total... I was as happy as anyone could possibly be. I longed for it again.

I placed the sun pendant gently on my cloth. Standing up I felt free in the night, with only the stars and the growing moon as my witnesses. I knelt stretching my arms before me and touched my forehead to the sand in surrender to Earthmother. Here I was, a single speck in the vast maze of Life. Nature was alive around me, yet I was so totally insignificant. Never had I been so alone.

I sat and locked my legs in the Lotus posture, my back comfortable and erect. I unwrapped from my wrist the length of twine Martal had given me.

"Tie fifty knots with a finger-width gap between them," he'd said, "then tie the ends together and place it around your neck like a necklace."

I had always imagined that Diipundi would conduct my Manhood Ritual. But Martal was one of the Shaktin adults I liked most and was always kind to our family. He had fought in the war with Father and was a fitting man to instruct me in the Manhood Ritual.

When I had asked him, he was a little hesitant and made the same point as Satu, "Patish, you should be trying not to draw attention to yourself, but I am proud of you and am honoured to instruct you in the Ritual."

One by one I tied the knots, counting to fifty as I went. I tied the ends of the string together and hung it over my neck. I was ready.

I held the string necklace in my left hand, pulling it along until I felt the large knot of the join, then held the next knot between my forefinger and thumb.

"Holding each knot," Martel had said, "and with your eyes closed, breathe in slowly through your nostrils. As you do this, do not think of anything, but allow thoughts to arise by themselves. As you breathe out through your nostrils, slowly, imagine that whatever thought you have at that moment is leaving you in your breath. If the thought of a mango arises as you breathe in, imagine that mango dissolving into your breath and leaving your mind as you gently breathe out. Imagine it merging into the vastness of the Universal Oneness."

I rested my right hand on my knee with my thumb touching the tip of my forefinger, ready to count.

"When you complete fifty breaths, that's one round of the knots, and you must do twenty rounds," Martel had said. "Count the rounds on your fingers and toes. The twenty rounds of fifty knots makes a total of a thousand. The last round, the twentieth, you complete with your palm open. It symbolises your openness, having given up everything of who you were, and your readiness to become who you truly are, to receive your destiny. You must do all this with your eyes closed. If for any reason, you open your eyes before completing the thousand breaths, you must start again at the beginning."

Closing my eyes, left hand holding the first knot, I began. As I took my first breath in, my mind had many thoughts at once: a sense of pride at what I was doing, I visualised myself sitting here, the feeling of the cool coarseness of the sand on my bare buttocks, and a soft ringing in my ears with gentle sounds of insects in the distance. The out breath was easier, and I imagined them all streaming out of my nostrils into the mysterious darkness of the Oneness from where all had come, and all things ended.

I moved my finger and thumb on to the next knot and breathed in slowly. This was harder than I had imagined, and, by the time I had completed breathing in, I hadn't really thought of anything, only felt a panic about whether or not I could do this. I breathed out, letting go of my tangled thoughts, letting them disappear into the dark nothingness. I moved my grip along the necklace knots and began my next in-breath. I focused on my breath, imagining the air coming into my nostrils and filling me with life. This worked and gave me a sense of control, which then became the thought I surrendered with my outbreath.

Before I knew it, I had reached the large knot of the join, completing the first round, which I counted on the large toe of my right foot. Still focused on my breathing, I became more relaxed about it and noticed my mind drifting off. Thoughts of Mother, Leeta and Seera arose, even as I breathed in and out. I wondered what they would think about what I was doing now.

Then I heard Seera's last loving words again, "I know you're the bravest in the land and you will come home, won't you?" And I saw her tears.

Now, I felt Mother's presence and almost opened my eyes.

"Patish," she said, "we miss you so much." I could hear the sob about to break in her voice. "Take care of yourself and remember, there is no higher duty, no higher honour than to look after your family."

I opened my eyes to embrace her, but she wasn't there. In the darkness, she was nowhere to be seen. Taking it all in – the dark shapes of the nearby trees, the distant horizon, the light sand of the riverbed – I realised I wasn't in Shaktin. Could I have been dreaming? I was sure I hadn't been asleep. I searched the sand for footsteps. There were none. Perplexed, I looked around again to make doubly sure. No one. I must have dozed into a dream.

I moved the string to the join, then held the first knot, while with my right hand I started again, my thumb touching my large toe. Annoyed with myself for opening my eyes, I determined not to let it happen again.

I began to let go of my thoughts as I breathed out, counting knots with my left hand, completing rounds of fifty on my toes with my right hand. Even as I breathed out my thoughts, sometimes I returned to thinking about the same thing. Other times I felt so still, almost like a statue, my breathing so light that I couldn't feel any expansion or contraction in my navel.

One time, my body felt out of control, almost floating or twisting around. It felt so real I wanted to open my eyes to see if I was still facing in the same direction. I resisted the temptation and let go of the thought with my out-breath. I continued in this way, breathing in with all sorts of thoughts arising, and breathing them out into the vastness beyond my imagination.

I had been through all sorts of thoughts of what had happened in the last few days, of Satu and my Shaktin brothers, of Mother, Leeta and Seera, of what I was doing now, where I was, and returning to the camp tomorrow. All these thoughts I kept breathing out, letting them go.

In the space of my meditative world, I remembered the dream I'd had yesterday afternoon of being at the well in Shaktin. A flush of heat came to my cheeks as I thought of Satu spilling the water and laughing every time I tried to fill my pot for Mother. Anger and frustration grew inside me. I breathed it all out, trying to let it go, but the anger still grew. Even though it had been a dream, Satu really had been trying to make me feel guilty for respecting Mother's wishes. I breathed out but couldn't let the thought go. Our friendship was being torn by my duty to Mother.

A deep sadness overcame me. Even my breathing failed to move it on. It was like falling down, deeper and deeper into a hole in the centre of my heart. I almost opened my eyes, but I regained some control by breathing out and feeling my fingers holding the knotted string. As I breathed in, the sadness overwhelmed me again, and I wondered about the last few days when my whole world had been thrown upside down. I missed the simple happiness of home and breathed out as tears rolled down my cheeks. In that moment of hopelessness, I heard a voice inside me say, "You are free, listen only to your heart..."

Was it my voice? I didn't know, but I let it sink in. "Listen to your heart..." These few words changed me. A wave of energy filled my soul and even my mouth felt sweet, as if I had just enjoyed a spoonful of honey. I breathed out, feeling that I had never felt more like I was truly myself. I knew that now I was a man.

My ears picked up a sound. Movement. Slow. Along the sand. Slithering. Heart beats thumped my chest. Snake. It was getting closer. I breathed out hoping it might disappear, but I knew it wouldn't. It was real and coming my way. A hundred thoughts. Stay calm. Any sudden movement, and it could attack. Might not even be dangerous, but if it was a large cobra, I would already be in its striking range.

It was right in front of me. I wanted to roll over sideways and run, but I didn't. Perfect stillness. Didn't breathe. Not even my navel moved.

A cool, flat serpent slid onto my thigh. Could this be it? Death?

I readied for the Unknown. I could taste my panic, but I stuck to stillness. Grains of sand got caught between our skins – tiny, course scratches interrupted its smooth caress. As it journeyed across my stomach, its powerful firmness turned and bent around my back. Was it wrapping itself around me?

The slithering continued on to the sand behind me as the rest of it followed its sliding path over my thigh, across my stomach and down behind my back. Then it was gone, as quickly as it had come. I listened to it disappear into the night. I breathed again. I could still feel its trail on my body. Sitting with my disbelief, I moved my left fingers to the next knot. It was a join. I felt my right finger counting – it was at my left thumb; I was onto my last round.

Resting the back of my hand on my knee, I felt the coolness of my open sweaty palm. I breathed out and let every thought of the snake – every fear and escape plan and the pride I was feeling at my bravery – dissolve away.

I remembered something Mother told us when Seera had seen a snake, and I had picked up a stick. Once when she was a little girl, a snake had wrapped itself around the neck of an Earthmother statue, like a garland of devotion. Her mother told her that even though most people fear and often hated snakes, Earthmother's love is so vast. She loves every creation. Even snakes.

Warm water welled in my eyes and streamed down my cheek. I, too, was part of Creation.

I knew that the snake was no accident, but a sign. I breathed out, overwhelmed by a sensation of love, not for anyone or anything in particular but for every living thing. It all made sense. Everything is alive, everything is connected – we are all just different forms originating from the One: Earthmother.

I completed the last round of knots. Elated, I sat in stillness and opened my eyes. Nothing around me had changed, but I had. I was ready to face the world. But I was also tired and ready for sleep. I hadn't eaten for a whole day and the thought of walking back didn't appeal. I clothed myself, hung Father's sun around my neck and lay down on my back. I looked up at the stars and the sliver of moon.

"Thank you, Mother," I thought as I closed my eyes and drifted off.

***

When I opened my eyes again it was to a day beaming with the sounds of life. Birds called and insects searched for food. Like them, I was hungry and keen to join the feast of the Manhood Ritual celebrations back at the camp.

I started walking, taking one last look at my sacred spot. White sand spread on either side of the shallow river, and visible in the distance, the rich green slopes of the valley and tablelands where Shaktin hid. I smiled a greeting to Mother, Leeta and Seera, turned and kept walking. In the vast blue sky above, a small white cloud floated, all alone.

Chapter 13: Tiger

Leeta

I couldn't get the thought of Limpy out of my head. All night I had tried to let go, to surrender all to Earthmother, to drift into the freedom of sleep, but I couldn't. That moment of him being struck down by the arrow... and later, Limpy's eyes, how they had still been open, the life inside him gone.

I wondered, could this be the complexity of death that Mother had never been able to fully explain to us? I'd been too young when we'd lost Father to think about the details of how it had happened. But now it seemed entirely strange that Patish and I had never discussed it. All that had mattered was that he was gone.

I opened my eyes. The morning light pierced the rainforest. Several brilliantly coloured red junglefowl flew through the treetops, singing with melodic, crisp notes as if to call the other creatures awake. I wished it was I that was so beautifully carefree.

I climbed carefully down from my makeshift tree bed to where Anula sat, frowning.

"Is everything alright?" I asked.

"Yes," she muttered. "I couldn't sleep. That's all."

"Nor could I. You look like you're guarding us from tigers or something."

"Actually, I feel like tigers are the least of our concerns today," she said, back to her sarcastic self. "I'm just not sure. Without the map and the Wisdom Wheel, how can we know we're going the right way?"

"We're moving uphill," I answered. "That's all we need to know. But," I paused, "we must be getting close to where the tigers roam."

"I remember Diipundi's warning," Anula said.

"Maybe you were right about the lost Wisdom Wheel," I reflected aloud. "The Mountain People may refuse to see us without it."

"Leeta, stop worrying, things will work out. Focus on the present, isn't that in your Way?"

I tried to answer, but she silenced me with a raised palm. "We need to start walking soon. The steeper this forest gets, the slower our climbing will become and we're running out of time."

I admired this new Anula. Witnessing Limpy's death must have changed her. Of course, she was right, we had to keep walking, even without the Wheel.

Anula reached into her bag and took out the sandalwood wax container. "I don't know how we forgot about this," she said nonchalantly. "I really don't think we're in prime tiger area, though."

She shrugged, took the lid off and rubbed some behind her ears.

"Thanks." I took the container and applied some on my forehead. "I'm ready. Let's go."

***

We soon reached a plateau where my feet were squelching in damp soil. I discovered a humble little spring oozing a trickle of water that disappeared under the forest mulch.

Stopping to enjoy the simple pleasure of cool dampness on my toes, something on the ground caught my attention. A paw print in the mud.

"Anula... look." I motioned with my hand. "Tiger's paw, and it's fresh!"

We scanned the surrounding trees, searching for signs.

"Listen, it's so quiet... no insects, nothing," I said.

Danger had sprung out of nowhere and yet was nowhere to be seen. My first instinct was to run. Escape, as fast as possible! But where to? I considered whether we could at least climb up a tree and hide.

"We could..." I began frantically, then stopped. There was no point in trying to out-run or out-climb the strongest and fastest predator in the whole forest.

Anula knelt beside the footprint and traced it with her forefinger. It was the same size as her hand. Though sweat glistened upon her brown skin, she shivered. "Do you think it's... watching us?"

I scanned the surrounds once more. We were at the opening of a clearing now. Large rocks broke up the continual maze of tree trunks and a small pool of water glittered from rays of sunshine penetrating the rainforest.

"I don't know," I murmured, still looking around.

"So, what do we do?"

I took a deep breath. This had always been my greatest fear. "If we find the tiger –"

"You mean, if the tiger finds *us*," Anula corrected.

"There's nothing we can do. We can't climb a tree..."

Anula's cheeks paled.

"We've still got the staff," she said.

Resisting the fear that tingled into my toes, I straightened my pack over my shoulder and took a step onto a crescent-shaped rock. Anula followed. The clearing was almost entirely rocky, covering what little water there was in the streamlet. I leapt from rock to rock, scanning the area ahead for tiger warning signs. Of course, I wasn't entirely sure what these were.

We reached a noisy trickle of water that splashed onto pebbles and into a narrow basin between the rocks. At the sight of the flowing water, I took out my water gourd and squatted, but I sprang backwards onto my feet again, making Anula – who was squatting beside me – fall backwards onto her bum.

"What!" she cried, looking around.

"Oh sorry, but one of us should keep watch, keeping the staff ready for defence," I said, squinting and looking through the trees.

Anula passed me the staff, returned her attention to the stream, and dipped her fingers into the water. She splashed the water up to her face, the cool relief immediately softening her features. After she drank, I handed her the staff.

I bent down, cupped a handful of water, and drank. After filling our water gourds without sign of a tiger, we began trekking uphill once more. Ancient trees engulfed us, and I felt extremely thankful to have Anula walking beside me.

"What do you actually know about the Purple Sage, Leeta?"

Was she just making conversation, or was she mocking me?

"Well, the Sage is wise and strong and always kind," I said, stepping over a fallen branch.

"No, no," Anula shook her head. Loose strands had escaped her tight plait and now fell softly over her face. "I mean, this whole trip is because you believe in the Sage..."

"Of course, I do," I said without thinking.

"So... do you really think the Sage will be able to help our brothers?"

"Yes," I said softly. "The Sage is often called The Wise One. His intelligence is known throughout the land." I knew I was just repeating what Diipundi always said. It seemed right. "The Sage will help us," I added with more certainty, keeping my eyes on the dark forest spaces.

To think that the Sage couldn't do anything for Patish... it was an unbearable thought, and I pushed it to the back of my mind.

"Be serious Leeta! You're just telling me what the Shaktin elders always say." She broke into a faster walk, brushing past me. "Think for yourself this time. What do you really believe?"

"You're walking too fast!" I responded. "We have to be careful." I wasn't sure whether I was avoiding her question on purpose or not.

Anula grimaced. "I am looking out for the tiger, Leeta, but we've probably lost him by now." She turned back to me. "So?"

"I've told you. That *is* what I really think."

"So, you really think the Purple Sage is the cleverest in all the lands?"

"Yes!" I spoke, not wanting to be challenged any further. I *had* to be right about the Sage. I couldn't even consider being wrong.

"But what could the Sage do for our brothers, truly, even if 'The Wise One' *is* the cleverest?"

"How am I meant to know?" I snapped. "That's why we're going! He'll know what to do."

Anula slowed her walking.

"So, what do *you* think about the Sage, then?" I asked her curtly. I knew Anula's ways only too well. She wouldn't be asking all these questions if she didn't have her own theories on the Sage that she wanted to divulge.

"I don't know," she started, "I really hope you're right. For Rakti's sake. But..." Her voice drifted.

"But?"

"Well, Diipundi sometimes said things about the Purple Sage that seemed... untrue. How would *he* know that the Purple Sage is the wisest in all the lands, when the Wise One has lived on some faraway mountain forever? Why would someone who is meant to be so powerful be hiding away? Maybe the Sage has a dark secret, a dark past, that Diipundi is keeping from us."

"What's your point?" My fingers curled into fists. It was one thing to be cynical, and another entirely to insult the spiritual Elder of our village.

"My point is, Leeta, that maybe the Sage won't be all that Diipundi has said. You should prepare yourself for that. It's like your Earthmother. Diipundi and the Elders always talk about Her influence, but, in the end, She's overseen the death of our fathers, and now our brothers are taken for war. Haven't you ever wondered about that?"

I was speechless. Anula was still talking, rambling. "See, Leeta, the Sage is not like the great warrior Ksanda, who fought and defeated Emperor Darius and the..."

I stopped listening.

I knew she didn't have the same beliefs as me, but her insensitivity! Anula didn't know what she was talking about. Of course, this mission was worth it. Diipundi was not a liar. Mother sent me for Patish, her only son. The Sage was going to help us. Anula was wrong.

"If you really think Diipundi and the Sage are such phonies, why did you even bother to come with me, Anula? Because your mother pushed you into it?" I was out of control, saying things that were meant to be only private thoughts. "Admit it – you've never wanted to be here, not from the start."

"Leeta, wait... I need to tell you something," she said, her eyes staring at the ground.

My eyes filled with angry tears. "Don't even bother making up silly excuses, because I know you don't really mean them."

Anula said nothing. I wiped my eyes with the back of my hand and waited. She was so quiet. I snuck a glance at her. Her mouth was slightly open, as if in shock, and her eyes were glassy. Just as a tinge of guilt filled my chest, Anula's lips opened further.

"Leeta," she croaked, "...*tiger.*"

Chapter 14: Bazzin the Fierce

Patish

Our drills were late, and while we waited, word spread that the prince was coming. An inspection or something. All you could hear now was talk about the prince.

Somehow, I never expected to actually see him. Maybe it was the way we were treated. Being a conscript was like being a prisoner or a slave. Obeying without a choice. We were reminded continually that it was both our duty and an honour to defend prince and country, but no matter how many times we were told, I still felt like a prisoner, here against my will. And it was the prince who was doing it to me. It was the prince who was causing the war. It was the prince who had sent his soldiers to drag us from our homes and families to this battlefield by the side of a holy river. And for what? Water, to grow his new crops of rice. The very water we had always shared with our neighbouring Pauravans, a kingdom we had always been friends with. It just didn't make sense.

As the blue head of an eagle rose and lent forward on the long bamboo flagpole, I started my routines of thrusting and parrying. To my surprise, I was imagining being watched by the prince. My thrusts were sharper and stronger than ever before, and even my grip on the lance was firmer. With every position, the muscles in my arms and legs felt like they had more power, and I realised that my anger with the prince was giving way to a fascination, not a new fascination but one that had lived within me for a long time. Like all the other boys, I loved the talk of heroes and legends; now I found myself captivated by the thought of seeing the young Prince of Gandhara. The talk was contagious, and the words kept repeating in my mind.

"He's a skilful swordsman and loves a duel."

"His father was a great warrior."

"He's only fourteen."

I vigorously whirled my cane, blocked, and thrust in one continuous motion. My movements really were energised by the thought of the prince watching me, and I was perplexed by my own desire to impress. It was only yesterday that I discovered my independence as a man, free to be myself and to determine my own destiny. Yet here I was with the same boyish wonder and fantasy, the same excitement I felt with Satu and our friends chasing monkeys in Shaktin.

I wondered about Rakti, and his story of saving the prince's life. Could it be true? Partially true? If it were, would the prince remember him? If it weren't, how would Rakti justify his story to us all? It would all come to a head now.

I imagined Rakti trying to approach the prince, a familiar face surfacing from a sea of soldiers' faces. The prince's guards would probably stop him before he even got close, and he would surely get a taste of Discipline after the prince had left.

But what if the prince did remember him? What if he did get transferred to the Royal Guard?

The thought of Rakti in the prince's own guard played on my mind. I couldn't help but think about the possibility of going with him. The more I thought about it, though, the more I realised just how unlikely it would be. It must have been years ago when he saved the prince, if it had ever happened at all. I remembered Satu's objections and felt stupid to even consider that the story could possibly be true. Grabbing a cobra with your bare hands!

I stepped sideways to avoid the deadly thrust of an imaginary enemy lance, ducked to dodge the follow-up swipe, then thrust to finish him off. The routine drill had become second nature already, and the possibility of going with Rakti just wouldn't leave my mind. The idea of leaving Mother and my sisters alone in the world, the thought of them having to face the news of me being killed in battle, was overpowering.

"Do anything to survive..." Mother's words came again, like they had just been spoken.

Bellowing conches and thumping drums in the distance stopped us all in the middle of our drills. We knew what it meant: the prince had arrived. Tall red flags stood at the heart of where every soldier looked. The very thought of seeing the prince seemed to excite everyone like children at a wedding feast.

I followed Janam, Laksa and Talbik as our flag led us into a huge gathering. The whole place was chaotic, with lines of red clad soldiers moving in from every direction. Order was restored by flag bearers forming a circle under the direction of a commander barking orders in the middle. We stopped in our tracks, trying to listen for orders at the same time as following our flag, should it start moving again. The centre of the circle was quickly cleared; this is where the prince would stop.

"We're lucky to be near the front," said Laksa, not taking his eye off the front in case the prince should suddenly appear.

"There's more and more arriving, must be half the Gandharan army coming here," said Talbik, who seemed more interested in the size of the gathering than the thought of seeing the prince.

"Those at the back will hardly see a thing," he added, grinning. But no one was really listening or wanting to make conversation. The excitement was enough.

Looking around, I spotted Sujas in the second row across the circle, then on my right, close to me, Tomay smiled and winked as he spotted me. Standing just in front of Tomay was Rakti. He looked nervous, and I guessed that he knew his game would be up; he would be exposed as a liar in front of us. Although I hadn't sighted Satu, I knew he would be watching, eager to have the final word.

"Told you so, don't know how you could have ever believed him," I could almost hear him saying, with Tomay, Sujas and the others all having a good laugh at my expense.

To my left, commanders were trying to open a path into the circle, motioning soldiers back with visible frustration. The soldiers were already packed closely together with nowhere to go, and the shouting of orders from so many at once just added to the confusion, making it impossible to know which order to follow. The chaos made me wonder what a real battle would be like, two whole armies merged in battle, with shouting and cries as metal tore flesh and blood spilt... Somehow, a clearing formed in the direction of two rows of tall red flags slowly heading our way.

Although we were close to the front, it was hard to get a good look at the prince. I barely caught a glimpse of him between a band of mounted generals, but what stood out most was the colour of his horse.

Black. I nearly choked on my own breath imagining Satu asking: "So, you rode the prince's white horse, did you?" but there was still no sign of him at all.

"Soldiers," boomed the unmistakable voice of Master Vinyak. "Salute your prince!"

With no idea of how to salute the prince, I copied the others. Everyone dropped to their knees, then lay face down with arms fully stretched towards the prince, foreheads touching the earth.

"Defenders of Gandhara, rise," the prince said. "It is an honour to be here with you today." His voice was confident but tender, and, though not what I had expected, it had a certain royal quality... that stirred my loyalty. I dusted myself as I stood up and, like everyone else, faced toward the prince and his generals.

As his horse stepped forward, Master Vinyak looked searchingly around before speaking. "I see our volunteers here looking truly like soldiers, even after only a few days of training. Who amongst them would like to demonstrate their combat skills for the prince?"

Everyone stood still, glancing around, as if hoping that someone else would volunteer. Murmurs broke across the circle and all eyes fixed on a sturdy young man with shaven head emerging from the mass of red.

"Ah, Bazzin," said Master Vinyak. "I'm sure you will put on a worthy display for Prince Ambhika and Minister Treviz – that is, if we can find anyone brave enough to take you on."

An unearthly silence broke out. Bazzin of Rolpur was well known to us from the Valley Games. I wondered if he was the elder brother of one of the Rolpur boys, hopefully not one who had been whipped. Satu had seemed afraid of the Rolpur boys when we last talked; now I could see why.

"Come, surely one of you champions is ready to bring fame to your village?"

None stepped forth.

Embarrassed, Master Vinyak tried again. "Whoever takes on Bazzin will have the choice of weapons."

Still there was silence.

"Well, then, Bazzin, choose an opponent."

Bazzin stalked slowly around the circle for someone to respond to his challenge. His hardened muscles rippled in the sunlight, and even his shiny head seemed to be one more powerful muscle that could easily destroy an opponent with a single head-butt. Everyone knew his reputation, and he seemed to enjoy this opportunity of displaying his supremacy in the presence of the prince. He eyed the onlookers who were mute with fear of being picked, but then someone called out, "Face like a rhino and a brain to match, none of us are that stupid!" Soldiers restrained their laughter, but it was enough to stir Bazzin's anger.

"Who was that? Come on, show me your courage instead of your voice!" he demanded.

Two boys from Rolpur stood behind Rakti, and one of them gave him a huge push so that he stumbled out in front of Bazzin, just managing to keep his balance.

"Good, now choose a weapon!" said Bazzin, his gaze fixed on Rakti. I knew that Rakti had no hope of defending himself. He had never joined our wrestling and combat games in Shaktin. His eyes were filled with terror and despair. He stuttered, gulping for air, trying to find the words he so desperately needed, but he was tongue-tied, the way I'd seen him react before. It was as if his thoughts disconnected with his voice when something like this happened.

I pushed forward through the line of soldiers in front of me and put my hand on Rakti's shoulder.

"Sorry, oh, great Bazzin," I said, "my friend didn't actually volunteer; he was pushed from behind. Please excuse him." I took hold of Rakti's arm and began to draw him back into the mass of disappointed spectators.

"Stop!" Bazzin jumped in front of me, "unless you want to take his place!" he ordered, glancing back toward Master Vinyak and the prince as if to confirm their approval. Master Vinyak gave an ever so slight nod. I realised then that I had no choice.

"You heard Master Vinyak, it's your choice of weapons," Bazzin said, not just offering me the choice, but commanding me to choose. He stood boldly, hands on his hips, as though this was some menial task he had to perform.

"Bare hands," I said, knowing I would have no hope with weapons. Bazzin frowned and again turned to Master Vinyak as if to question my choice.

"I gave him the right to choose," Master Vinyak said, the authority in his voice final. Bazzin turned to me, his eyes now focused on me with intent, his face undergoing a transformation as he took small steps and crouched toward me like a tiger ready to spring. From behind, arms pushed me further into the clearing. I stood there facing the meanest face I have ever seen.

A chant broke out all around.

"Ba-zzin! Ba-zzin! Ba-zzin!"

Instinctively, I crouched too. Bazzin spun as if in a dancing twirl. As he completed the spin, up flew his foot and caught me square on the shoulder, knocking me off balance and flat to the ground. He could've taken advantage and finished me then and there, but no, that would've been too easy. He was relishing the moment, and he wanted to play. He stood straight, with a proud smirk across his face, motioning me with his hand to get up.

The chant broke out again, with even more vigour.

"Ba-zzin! Ba-zzin! Ba-zzin!"

Loving the cheers and laughter of the crowd, he crouched again, the hardened look on his face more sinister than ever, a rhino about to charge. I knew there was only one way I had any hope to take on this monster.

I stepped toward him, crouching with my head stuck out low, an offering I hoped he could not resist. Sure enough, Bazzin flew forward to take the bait, his left arm sweeping around the back of my head to apply a headlock.

Before he could close the hold, I swung my right arm over his shoulder and across the side of his face, then sprang up with all my might, using my left hand to leverage my right arm. This hold had always worked, but I had never felt a neck so strong. It was thick like the neck of a buffalo, but as I applied every bit of strength I had, I pulled my head free and simultaneously extended my arms as hard as I could. Bazzin fell helplessly to his knees, his shoulder blade wedged dangerously up near to his ear as I increased the pressure and pushed him down to the ground. His muscular body struggled against my hold, but his own force worked against him to increase the pain.

Although I had him, I knew what he would do if he managed to free himself. The humiliation would enrage him, and I would be in even more danger. I released the hold and jumped to my feet.

"Oh, Great Bazzin," I said loudly, "you are truly humble in your greatness, teaching me a reverse headlock lever, a hold I will never forget and will apply against the prince's enemies. Thank you for the lesson, oh, Great one." I knelt and bowed as if acknowledging the victor.

Bazzin rose, confused. I stood to face him, not knowing how he would react. If he chose to keep fighting, I was in serious danger. A sickly weakness passed through my stomach and my knees.

At that moment, out of the crowd jumped Satu with the look of a boy facing his hero, waving his arms to the crowd as he started a chant. "Bazzin the Great, teacher by example! Ba-zzin! Ba-zzin!" And the crowd joined in, blindly, probably not even realising what had actually happened.

His pride recovered, Bazzin raised his arms in the air, victor.

Martal appeared from nowhere and grabbed my arm, leading me away through the crowd as all eyes focused back on the prince.

Martal and I sat down on rocks under the shade of a peppercorn tree near the riverbank, well away from the events of the Royal visit. Perplexed by just how Satu and Martal had mysteriously intervened to help me escape any further challenge, I asked him "How did you and Satu…" but, before I could continue, Martal smiled and cut me off mid-sentence.

"When I saw Bazzin choose Rakti, and then you when you stepped in to help him, I knew I had to do something. Over the years, I've seen Bazzin maim opponents without a care. It means little to him to break someone's bones or to leave them scarred for life. I had been standing near Satu and told him to be ready, that we would have to do something. I nearly jumped in after Bazzin knocked you down, but I saw you begin your feint… I knew how well you could apply that hold, so I decided to wait."

I was proud to hear Martal say that, and felt a smile cross my face. I thought of how often Martal had helped Diipundi with our lessons in the defensive arts, and that he must be feeling pleased with himself too. Martal seemed to reflect for a moment, and then looked at me again intensely.

"Patish, you showed great courage in supporting Rakti, and your wrestle with that..." checking to see if anyone else could hear, "beast Bazzin today was a real mark of a man, but... there's something I really need to talk to you about. In that bout, your safety hung in the balance, but your Nature came through for you. That's what I saw in you today, your Nature, so much like your father's!"

No one had ever said that to me before.

"You are so much like your father, more than you could imagine," he went on, again making sure no one could hear before continuing. "Patish, you should have broken Bazzin's arm when you had the chance... or his neck. Because now, he will seek you out, and if he gets his opportunity, he will crush you without mercy. Wise you were to publicly deny your victory, and that may gain you a little time, but everyone knows you beat him, and he is not one to accept humiliation, especially from one so young. And when he finds out you're from Shaktin... Don't trust him for a moment, and don't believe yourself safe at any time, even in the battlefield. He has a nasty heart and won't rest until he traps you in some cunning situation where he is sure to win. You must keep away from him, and look out for his cronies too, especially the cross-eyed one they call Slicer."

I heard his warning, but my mind was elsewhere.

"Tell me again, Martal, how am I like my father?" Mother never talked about Father and had never mentioned that I was like him.

Martal's eyes avoided mine.

"Please, Martal, tell me," I said, praying he wouldn't just dismiss it the way adults do when they don't want to answer.

"Patish, when I saw you defeat Bazzin, it was as if I was watching your father in battle. I saw your father die, and I tell you this for your own good. Your father Rewold had the courage of a tiger and the strength of a buffalo, and he could move as quick as a mongoose. Yet, like you, he was a gentle man with a heart of compassion, and without hatred. I never heard him say a bad word about anyone, and he lived the Way of Peace as truly as anyone I know. But, when we were conscripted and there was no choice, his bravery was second to none.

"When the battle started, Rewold was in the front line with our champions and engaged a mighty warrior in a fight as fierce as any I have seen. When your father stood above this warrior with raised sword, he stopped and lowered it, unable to complete the kill. Another enemy warrior saw his back turned and spared not a thought in taking his life, his mace felling him with a crushing blow to the side of his head."

I gasped, staring at Martal but picturing Father's death in my mind.

Martal paused and held my hand. "I tell you this Patish," he said. "On the battlefield there is only one choice: kill or be killed. I tell you this because I have seen you grow up as a child and never have I seen you kill a helpless bird or frog; your eye is sharp and your aim is true, but, whenever the boys have had a living target, I noticed that your stones have gone astray.

"Your mother – and your father, for those few years – have raised you in the spirit of the Way, of Nature and Compassion, and your heart is pure, like few others. But, on the battlefield, Patish, there are no choices if you want to stay alive, and it is your duty to your mother to do so."

I sat, silent, taking in Martal's words.

"Patish, I did not mean to upset you," Martal said, placing his hand on my shoulder. "What are you thinking? Speak your feelings."

"The last thing Mother said to me was 'do everything you can to survive'," I said, "and now I understand her words. I have been puzzled all along since we left Shaktin, not knowing what to do. Mother has always taught me to respect living things and to love life even more than I love her. How confusing life is!"

"Patish, this war is not of your making, nor of mine. We are like horses now, without freedom to act as we wish, with no alternative but death on the battlefield at the hands of the enemy, or death at the hands of our own soldiers if we refuse to fight."

Chapter 15: The Tiger's Trap

Leeta

I searched the landscape before us, the canopy of twisted trees, the fallen vines, the green clump of bamboo to our right, as Anula pointed.

Thirty or forty paces from us was a sly movement of thick black stripes, visible when a breeze parted the grasses. With a couple of giant strides, a tiger emerged fully and crouched low. It wasn't hiding. Muscles rippled under its thick orange coat and gleaming yellow eyes stared right into mine.

It was fixed on me.

The previously quiet forest burst into a frenzy of noise. In the trees, monkeys screeched, foraging birds fluttered, and something hidden by the grass scurried away through the fallen leaves.

The tiger did not move.

The forest quietened once more. Dead quiet.

"Could it... could it just be curious?" Anula asked quietly.

No, it couldn't, I answered in my head. This was a tiger on the prowl. We were the prey.

"Don't talk," I hissed. "I keep telling you how intelligent animals are, but you never get it – listen, see how they've all gone silent? We must do the same."

"Then why are you talking?" she hissed back. "And they haven't gone silent; they've run away!" Anula beckoned to the trees. She was right. We were the only ones left.

I did not dare turn away from the predator. The tiger's eyes were still fixed on us, and for a moment I was enchanted by its strange beauty. Its presence was as imposing and terrible as it was majestic. This was the strongest, most dangerous thing I had ever seen.

Anula edged closer. "What do we do?" Her voice was pure terror.

I had no answer. The bamboo staff that she held bravely toward the tiger would be a useless defence. Running backwards and away would create a chase that we would lose. This is what hopeless felt like.

"Leeta, I have to tell you something: I lied to you. You deserve to know the truth. Before it's too late."

"What do you mean?"

Without realising it, I turned to look at her, breaking eye contact with the tiger. What could she have lied about?

Staring at the clump of bamboo behind her, I remembered Diipundi's advice. "Anula! The bamboo!" I grabbed her hand and slowly pulled her forwards.

We edged toward the clump of thick green bamboo and paused. The tiger did not stir.

I took three slow, measured steps. We were almost in the safety of the bamboo...

"LEETA!" Anula screamed as the tiger leapt out from the grass and bounded toward us.

"QUICK!" I hauled Anula with me in between a clump of the thickest bamboo stems, weaving my own body backwards in between the maze of stalks.

I could hear the tiger's breath. Heavy, hungry. We pushed our way deeper in amongst the bamboo. The tiger pushed its head against the stems. It was too big – its massive jaws were too wide to fit between the densely growing bamboo.

I sucked in my breath and rotated my shoulders to squeeze even further back into the clump. The tiger's face was only an arm's length away. In its black pupils, I could see my own reflection. Trapped for its dinner. But safe, at least for the moment.

Unable to penetrate the bamboo, the tiger lifted its right leg, pawing the bamboo to see if it could be knocked down, but its claws merely scratched the hard surface.

"Did the Purple Sage plant this bamboo?" Anula murmured in my ear from where she crouched, jammed amongst the bamboo directly behind me.

"Yes."

A cautious smile emerged on Anula's lips, and I knew exactly what she was thinking. Smart. That's smart! Because of the intelligence of the Sage, we had been saved.

The thought reignited a spark of hope that shimmered and sparkled in my mind.

"What if the tiger never leaves?" Anula whispered. "We can't stay here forever."

"Surely, it'll just get hungry and leave."

The tiger was doing no such thing. It settled on the ground a few paces away. Waiting.

"Oh no," Anula breathed.

We would be here all night, and that was if we were lucky. I let my tense shoulders drop and my head lean against the bamboo behind. It was extremely uncomfortable jammed in so tightly. I was already feeling squashed and claustrophobic.

Maybe the bamboo had only delayed our suffering. I clutched one of the thick stems and squeezed. Again, hope was fading.

It just seemed wrong. How could we be so close to the Purple Sage to have everything end now? Was this really what Earthmother had intended for me? For my family? The total injustice was impossible to comprehend. I'd strived to be kind and honest, to be a good person... and I had total faith in Earthmother, and yet... here we were.

"Maybe you were right, Anula," I said softly into the darkening forest.

"About what? "

"You know. That I have too much faith in things." The truth was out in the open.

"No." The gentleness of Anula's voice surprised me. "No, Leeta. I wish I had as much belief and confidence in life as you," she sighed. Which reminded me – she had been about to tell me something before.

"What was it that you were going to say earlier?"

Anula went quiet. I waited. Night was coming. Already, I could not see much beyond the closest tree to the bamboo clump. But I could still make out the tiger's presence, now just a large shadow on the forest floor.

Anula broke her silence. "Leeta, I didn't come with you on this journey to help you reach the Purple Sage," she paused. I waited. What was she saying?

"I came because... I came to stop you." Her voice was shaky, but her words rang clear. I couldn't understand. It didn't make sense. Stop me? Why?

Anula cleared her throat and continued, her voice so restrained it was as if she were standing a long way away. "When Mother heard your plan to seek the help of the Sage, she saw an opportunity to make a deal with the chief minister of the prince. I didn't really think it through, Leeta, I just agreed to it."

"What? I don't understand. What deal?"

"Mother said that the chief minister..."

"Who's that?" I asked, trying to understand what on earth she was talking about.

"He's the advisor of the prince, you know... the prince is young, and he's guided by Minister Treviz... so Mother will go to Taxila. She's probably been there by now to tell Minister Treviz about the Sage. And for a reward she will ask him to move Rakti to the palace guards so he doesn't have to fight in the battle."

"Stop, you're talking too quickly," I commanded. "You came on this mission to stop me reaching the Sage, because of a secret deal to save your brother?"

"Yes," she confessed. Her words were sharp as knives. "And then when we heard the assassins' plan yesterday, to kill the prince AND the palace guards, I knew I'd been wrong. The plan had been so wrong."

"How dare you!" I growled. "You've been trying to sabotage me this whole time? Are you serious?"

"I didn't think of it like that. Mother asked me! Leeta, I'm so sorry, you have to believe me."

"Right, because orders are orders. I've heard that one before! You think 'sorry' is going to make this all better? I trusted you! I thought you were my friend!"

"No, no, I mean it, Leeta. We are friends!"

"That's easy to say now, isn't it?" I fumed. "I knew that there was some reason you always had it in for me, but I never expected that you'd planned something so nasty... we're meant to be Spirit Sisters! What a joke that you ever took that vow!"

"Leeta I, I –" Anula stuttered. I didn't know what to think. She was a liar. No, worse than that. A traitor. She didn't have the right to justify herself now.

"What about Patish?" I let the fury break into my voice. "Did you ever think about that? Did you ever even consider that my brother would probably die going along with your plan? Is that what you wanted, to see me and my family suffer again?"

"Of course not! Listen –"

"No, I'm not listening to you! I don't even know who you really *are*! You were a coward not to stand up to your mother! You knew the consequences. I thought you were so much more than that."

Anula began to cry; I didn't care at all. "And now? Now that we're going to be a tiger's breakfast? You got your wish. I'm sure your mother will be *so* proud that we never reached the Sage."

I was done. I would not talk to Anula ever again.

I looked out into the darkness. In my next breath, I swallowed the reality of the betrayal. It hurt to lose a friend, even though I never really knew the real her. It hurt knowing now that I had brought this on myself with such a naive plan. It hurt even more knowing that it was all over. I had failed my loved ones and would never see them again.

My chest heaved with raw sobs that took over. I pressed my head against the bamboo, closed my eyes and surrendered myself to fate. The tiger, the supreme predator of the forest, lay there in the blackness of night, waiting.

Chapter 16: The Palace Guards

Patish

I couldn't get used to being treated like a hero, and they weren't letting up. Even conscripts I didn't know were calling me by name, telling me how they'd cheered for me, hoping I would defeat Bazzin. Whenever I tried to say how lucky I was, they dismissed it immediately. Janam was especially lively, taking every opportunity for a laugh.

"How good was that hold, defeating the monster within the blink of an eyelid. One moment he was a raging rhino, the next he was a bleating goat, submitting to the power of our mighty Patish!"

"Janam," I pleaded, knowing it was pointless, "I told you it was just a hold I knew..."

He wouldn't hear a word of it and motioned with his hands towards the mountains.

"When this quiet boy from the peaceful Shaktin rubbed the face of that monster Bazzin into the dirt while the prince and all the generals of Gandhara watched, I swear I saw the Gods peaking over the top of Naked Mountain, smiling at the courage and the skill of their modest son and cheering him on!"

Laksa, Talbik and the others sitting nearby all burst into laughter again, and I couldn't help cracking a smile. The thought of the Gods peaking over the mountains was pretty funny. It must have spurred him on – he was really enjoying having an audience. He stood and walked around this time as he prepared to shower me in his witty praise again.

"Who knows, perhaps the Pauravans have called off the war after hearing of the valour of our Champion from Shaktin. And if they haven't, sure defeat awaits them and anyone who dares stand in his way!"

I cringed, burying my face in my hands as the others laughed again.

"I can just see it happening," said Talbik, wanting a bit of the limelight. "The Pauravans attack and Janam steps forward, no weapon in his hands, and starts rambling on about the might of a young Nature-worshipping villager in our ranks. The Pauravans drop to their knees and roll over with laughter, and we claim victory!"

I couldn't stop the laughter this time, it was a real belly laugh, I just let go and enjoyed it. It was the first real laugh I'd had since arriving here. It put me so at ease, and I couldn't help thinking again how much these new friends were like my brothers of Shaktin.

As I waited for the next round of jokes, I saw the smiles drop from the faces of Janam, Talbik and Laksa. For a moment, I thought I had said something wrong, but then I realised that they were not looking at me but behind me. I turned to see four soldiers approaching, none of whom was familiar. They carried no weapons and wore no belts, just soldiers off duty, like us.

"Judging from the celebratory atmosphere, this must be the unit of the champion Patish," said the one at the front, a wiry man who had one eye that constantly looked sideways.

"I am Patish, but I am no champion," I said, facing him, wondering what they wanted.

"Humility is the mark of true greatness, my friend. We would truly be honoured if you would join us in a game of Kabbadi."

There was something about these soldiers that made me uneasy, but before I could think about it, Janam stood up and answered.

"Of course! We accept. It'll be the young and the quick, against the stout and the strong." Janam expected more laughter, but no one laughed. I didn't really feel like a game of Kabbadi under a challenge from unknown adults, yet I didn't want to offend them, especially after Janam's acceptance. But their leader lost no time in responding.

"Excellent. Now that the high heat of the day has passed, let us take to the field before anyone else claims it."

Without another word, Laksa and the others were up and around me, keen to meet the challenge, and itching to make a name for themselves too. As we walked past the other tents, the onlookers seemed to understand what was happening and fell in behind us.

"Kabbadi challenge," they whispered. The echo of their words travelled faster than our steps and now the other conscripts were coming too. I saw Tomay and Sujas join in, then, amongst the next group, Satu and Asten.

"We're right here with you, Patish," said Satu as he joined in next to Laksa. I smiled my acknowledgement to him and to Asten, who I was surprised to see.

"Great to have you all in my team," I said. "Haven't seen much of you lately, Asten."

"I was with my father at first, but they decided to put me back with my own age group and now I'm in Satu's unit," he said, walking proudly next to Satu as he had so often done in Shaktin.

We reached the field to see there was already another small crowd waiting.

"Patish, can I be on your team?"

Just about every conscript wanted to play, but I had already decided to include all my Shaktin brothers as well as Laksa, Janam, Talbik and the others from our unit to make up our team of twelve.

As we gathered in a circle to plan our tactics, a young voice interrupted. It was Liddu in his red and white messenger's uniform.

"Patish, I must speak to you," he said, pushing into our group.

"Liddu, sorry I didn't see you before, but I've already picked the team," I said, knowing he would be disappointed.

"No, you don't understand," he said, catching his breath.

I could see now that he had been running.

"It's a trick... to get you. Bazzin, and Slicer... one of my friends, a messenger, overheard them plotting..." Liddu paused for breath, a real look of fear on his face.

"Bazzin is going to get you during the game," and he turned around, motioning with his eyes and forehead towards the challenging team. Sure enough, removing a red shawl from his glistening head was the unmistakable figure of Bazzin.

It is amazing how quickly things can change. Like a deadly storm that comes from nowhere, this place had totally changed in a matter of a few words. I stood in shock. What was going to be a fun-filled game of daring and chases was suddenly a battlefield, a field for revenge, and the target was me. There would be no stopping him once the contest began. I knew Martal had warned me with good reason.

Bazzin's reputation was built on the shattered bones of his victims. And the danger wasn't only to me, but to my closest friends.

"I'm calling it off," I said to my team.

"What? You surely don't mean it," said Janam. "Where has all your courage gone? That big ox and his old friends will never match our speed." He cracked a grin, but no one laughed.

"We're standing with you whatever you decide," said Satu.

"You don't understand…" I was about to tell them what Liddu had revealed, but I stopped. Word might get back to Bazzin that Liddu betrayed him and that would put Liddu in real danger.

"Doesn't take much to shake up you Shaktin boys!" Janam said with a smirk.

Satu lurched toward him, but Laksa was quick enough to step in with his hands up.

"Sorry for that… he didn't mean it… talks without thinking sometimes. I think I understand what's going on here, and now I see your wisdom. I've heard about Bazzin's reputation, and it would be foolish to face him knowing the grudge he bears you… and us."

Janam dropped his eyes to the ground.

Laksa was a quick thinker and summed it up well. "But how do we call it off in front of everyone? And what if his friends want to hold us to our word? It would give cause for them to be offended."

"You are right," Satu said. "It isn't that easy to go back on one's word. If they look like they're getting dangerous with Patish, we all get in, right?"

Satu's words of loyalty were those of the brother I knew, and I nodded my appreciation. I had a bad feeling about this but was lost for words. Satu had already accused me of being a coward when I had talked about the royal guards, so I couldn't let him think it again. I couldn't see any way out.

We lined up for the game. As we faced Bazzin, Slicer and their team, the sound of hooves rose from the earth as though Mother Earth herself was intervening. Never did I expect to be so glad to see Master Vinyak. Into the centre of the Kabbadi field, he rode with Commander Rixten and four palace guards in their easily recognisable uniforms.

"That's Patish," a familiar voice cried out. It was Rakti, riding double behind one of the palace guards. They came to a halt, and Master Vinyak looked at us.

"Well, young Patish, it looks as though I've come at a good time." He turned to face Bazzin. "You should be ashamed of yourself, plotting revenge to restore your pride. I've heard of your tactics in Kabbadi, and there is no way I will allow it against these young conscripts. This is a matter for Discipline. What is it with you villagers of Rolpur?" He freed the bullwhip from his saddle and threw it at my feet.

"Patish, pick up the whip. This man has baited you and your friends so he can break your bones and get away with it under the pretext of a game. Bazzin, remove your top and turn your back to the boy."

All of this happened so fast I could barely think, but one thing I knew was that I could never whip anyone, not even Bazzin.

"Master," I said, leaving the whip in the dust. "As you know, I am from Shaktin and a follower of The Way. You mentioned that Bazzin was seeking revenge, but if I were to whip him now, would I not be guilty of the same thing? The Purple Sage has said that forgiveness is a greater force than revenge. I ask your permission to show forgiveness instead."

Master Vinyak frowned. "You have wisdom beyond your years. I grant you your wish, but I do ask Bazzin what he can give you in return."

"If you permit, I ask for his friendship," I said. I turned from the great general to Bazzin.

Bazzin bowed his head.

"Take your friends to your quarters and don't even think about coming back here again," ordered Master Vinyak on his horse, back straight, eyes unflinching. He was the supreme commander, commanding supremely.

Bazzin glanced at me, picked up his shawl and walked away with his friends.

Master Vinyak turned his horse to face me. "Patish, get your things from your unit. You and Rakti are going to join the palace guards."

What? I stood for a moment trying to make sense of it all.

Satu pieced it together though and turned to me: "Rakti! It was true after all!" Then, with a look of scorn more hurtful than anything he had ever said or done, he added, "And that's why you protected him!"

Before I could say a word, he turned and walked away.

***

Riding a horse was much less comfortable than I had ever imagined. Like most boys in Shaktin, I'd only ridden on the back of a buffalo when ploughing the fields. I held the hips of the palace guard as I sat behind him, half on his saddlecloth and half on the bare brown skin of the horse's back, bouncing up and down as it jogged along. With my pack strapped to my back and my legs dangling freely, I must have been quite a sight, for the other palace guards kept glancing over at me as they rode, probably expecting me to fall off.

Rakti, in spite of his claim to having ridden the prince's horse, appeared even sillier than I imagined I did, bouncing up and down and clinging like a child to the soldier in front of him.

I didn't know what to make of this new situation; my thoughts just kept bouncing around. One moment I was angry with Rakti for what he had done, the other I was thankful for being saved from the revenge of Bazzin. But most confusing was joining the Palace Guard. This was the very thought I'd had after Rakti had told us his story of saving the prince – and now it had actually happened. Satu was shocked. So was I. I couldn't get his angry words out of my mind. Maybe he was right. Maybe it was the reason I had protected Rakti?

I was glad it wasn't long before we reached Taxila. A set of stone steps announced the edge of the walled city, and I could see how in the wet season the river would flood and the bottom steps would be close to the edge of the water. Beyond the steps rose buildings taller than trees, their walls like hardened sand with windows and grand doorways adorned with carvings and colour.

Rakti and I were let down off the horses to walk behind the guards. I didn't say anything to him. I still wasn't sure whether I was angry at what he had done, or whether I should be thanking him, possibly for saving my life. I wanted to understand him, but he didn't seem interested in talking to me, acting as though everything happening was just normal. It was just like in Shaktin where on rare occasions he would mingle with us yet seem to stay in his own world until there was something he wanted to exclaim or to complain about. His simplicity made him a misfit as far as the rest of us were concerned, but I accepted his difference and knew he wasn't at all stupid. His skill with a knife was extraordinary, and he could sculpt the likeness of an animal out of the most useless piece of wood.

Up the steps, through a guarded archway, we entered a whole new world. I marvelled at the buildings, all built in straight lines, one next to the other on both sides of the road. The smell of incense burning for the deities of small shrines sweetened the air, but it was also full of odours of roadside dung and human sewage that flowed along the brick ditch in the middle of the road.

We soon came to a marketplace where the buildings surrounded a large open square. Everything you could imagine was being sold; baskets of fruits, vegetables, grains and spices covered the ground; earthen pots stood up, small and large in every conceivable shape, elegant and bulky; earrings, necklaces, trinkets of metal and polished stones, knives and blades in more sizes and designs than I had ever seen lay spread out on blankets; and tables with rolls of brilliant fabrics that looked like they had stolen their colours from Mother Nature's brightest of flowers.

Cows and dogs wandered randomly through, scavenging from the litter that speckled the earth. There were lots of people, mostly women and children, and the only men to be seen, apart from soldiers, were those too old for the army, and holy men in their saffron robes. Among them were voices speaking languages from other lands, traders whose goods flowed into the street, carried on heads, in bullock carts, or packed onto mules and camels and any other creature that could bear the burden. Life in the city went on busily even without the men of Gandhara who were in the training camps by the river, preparing for war.

On the other side of the square, we stopped at an entrance protected by guards. I knew this must be the palace. The gate was of solid timber and metal, and it looked like it could withstand the charge of a hundred rhinos, yet it was covered with intricate carvings and metallic decorations that formed a giant image of a sacred peacock, its tail open like a fan. I couldn't help but think of this strange quirk, for, when the peacock fully opens its feathers, rainfall is on the way. Yet this very prince was about to go to war for water.

Inside the walls, we entered an even more beautiful world. I had heard the word "paradise" before but never really understood what it meant. My eyes feasted on a garden bigger than all of Shaktin.

Paved pathways and steps led into courtyards with statues of gods and animals, huge pots exploding with plants, and raised ponds with sculptures from which water poured. Peacocks and long-legged water birds roamed freely and there beyond a line of mango trees was a building that could only have been created by the gods. Its sandy shades were like a golden temple rising from the centre of a luscious field. I stood in awe of the beauty and recalled a moment when Diipundi had seen me admiring the beauty of a pink lotus in bloom.

"Beauty is but one of the changing faces of Nature," he said. "When you admire the beauty of a lotus, don't forget to appreciate the beauty of the mud in which it grows."

I wondered if he had ever seen what I was seeing, and what he would say if he were here right now.

"Patish, amazing, isn't it?" Rakti said proudly, like he belonged here.

"This is where we lived, over there in the workers' huts," he said, pointing to a corner, "before we moved back to Shaktin."

"Come, I will take you to your quarters," a palace guard said.

We picked up our packs and followed him to a large building that was joined to the palace wall.

Chapter 17: Mountain People

Leeta

Was colour ever so bright and alive? Had the rays of sunlight beaming through the trees always been so sharp? What they revealed was surely heaven.

The tiger was gone.

Upon waking, I wondered whether I was alive or in some sort of after-life. I nudged Anula who was still asleep, slumped awkwardly against the bamboo.

She woke with a start, squinting her way into the world, and then gasped, her mouth stretched wide into a smile. "We're here! The tiger has left!"

We grabbed each other's hands and wriggled our way out of the bamboo. Together we danced into the light.

"Thank you, Mother!" I sang into the forest.

"Thank you, Tiger!" Anula yelled, scaring a bird that screeched and took flight.

"Thank you, bamboo!" I screamed, taking giant exaggerated steps over to the plantation and gave it a huge hug.

"Thank you, night!" Anula cried.

"Thank you, day!" I copied.

"Thank you, earth!" Anula bent down and kissed the dirt.

"Thank you, rocks!" I picked one up and threw it into the air.

Anula caught it. "Why thank you rocks?"

"I don't even know!" I laughed, a laugh so free that Anula caught it too, and we collapsed into the ferns, happy tears rolling into our open mouths, crying, and laughing as the forest morning began.

Finally, I sat up, and, as I did, the previous night's events flooded back into my mind. When I looked at Anula, she giggled, then realised from my changed expression what I had just remembered.

Her body language shifted dramatically as she sat up and pulled her knees into her chest, staring at the ground. I waited for her to speak.

"Leeta," she said very quietly. "Please forgive me. Maybe I don't deserve any compassion, but I'm wholly sorry... I was so confused. I wanted Mother to be proud of me, so I thought that if I did this..." She met my eyes and took a deep breath. "Do you think we could start this again? We can still reach the Purple Sage and save both our brothers... together?"

I glanced behind me into the twisting of trees and vines and darkness.

"We can't keep the Mountain People waiting too much longer," I whispered.

Anula brushed away a little tear and stood beside me.

I took her hand and she squeezed it. We had brothers to save.

***

From the thick tree roots woven and twisted into the shape of a bridge that crossed a deep gully, we could tell we'd reached the land of the Mountain People.

Anula volunteered to cross first without fear of the long drop below. I wondered if I really knew her. Having lived in the wilderness for the past few days, we were comforted to think we would soon be in the safety of friends.

"Smoke," I said, sniffing. "Must be a village nearby."

Small signs along the path were carved into the trees but in symbols we could not recognise. Soon we could hear the squeal of children's laughter, and then we saw a group of children playing on the outskirts of a clearing. Anula grabbed my drape and pulled me behind a tree.

High above, some monkeys started chattering loudly, almost laughing.

"Shhhhh," I said, trying to quieten them before they gave us away.

"Leeta, one more thing I need to tell you," Anula confessed. "I lost the Wisdom Wheel on purpose. I took it out of your bag and left it under a rock when you were asleep."

"I *knew* I hadn't lost it!" I said. "Anything else you want to tell me?"

"I'm sorry. So, now, we've got to find some other way of showing we come in peace and seek the Purple Sage."

I peeked out from behind the tree. Not unlike Shaktin at midday, villagers were busy making lunch arrangements, talking quickly in a dialect I didn't understand.

"Does something about this place seem weird to you?" Anula asked softly.

"Compared to Shaktin, of course it looks weird. The people seem happy – they have no war to fear. And the men and boys are still with their families."

I thought of Patish and Seera at the well.

"Look, let's just go in and try to explain," I said. "We can't stay hidden forever. We'll think of some way to communicate."

"No, you wait here," ordered Anula, "while I go and try to talk to them. That way, if something happens to me, you can go on. Got it?"

Now Anula was being heroic.

"But—"

"I owe you many times over, Leeta."

Anula started heading toward the village. She didn't get far. Out of nowhere a mob of Mountain People with spears encircled her.

Chapter 18: My Friend, the Prince

Patish

We had barely changed into our new red and blue uniforms when a well-groomed palace guard appeared.

"Is that how I look now?" I thought, reimagining myself.

"Patish?" he asked. "Prince Ambhika commands your presence."

Rakti stepped forward.

"No, not you," the guard pronounced. "Only the one by the name of Patish."

Mystified, Rakti sat down, gazing at the ground.

My head swirled with a thousand questions as I followed the guard through the garden and up rows of steps to a door. This door was a smaller version of the mighty palace gate, but just as solid and even more beautifully decorated. Carvings, paintings, and metallic pieces again formed the same picture of a peacock with tail feathers open in a proud display.

Two guards, one on either side of the door, stood like statues, holding tall lances with a red silky ribbon that drooped from the height of the metal spearhead. Slowly and silently, the door swung open, and we entered a mysterious, shadowy darkness filled with aromatic scents. It was cool as an early pre-dawn morning and the only light came from oil lamps that flickered to reveal rows of smooth stone pillars with carvings of deities between them. You could get lost in here and never find your way out, I thought.

I followed the guard to an area that was more brightly lit by hundreds of oil lamps sitting on tables, fixed to the walls, and suspended by chains from the ceiling.

"Wait here," the guard whispered. "When the prince appears, prostrate yourself until he commands you to rise."

I nodded. Right now, I would just about agree to anything.

After a few moments, a figure in a long white gown and a pure white turban entered the room. I felt a push on my shoulder and immediately dropped to the floor, my arms outstretched and my forehead touching the cool stone floor.

"Patish, that's your name, isn't it? Rise."

I recognised the prince's voice. It was young and authoritative, yet soft and friendly. I stood to face him and felt like I was facing a mythical god. The fine white cloth of his gown and turban glowed from the light of the oil lamps, and his eyes glittered like the golden necklace that hung around his neck.

"Yes, ahh, your Majesty," I said, not knowing how to address him.

"Guards," he said, "leave us be." They immediately left.

"Just call me Ambhi... at least when we're alone," said the prince. "But they'll probably flog you if you address me like that in public," he added, laughing. "I hope you don't mind being transferred to my guards?"

"Of course not, Your Majesty..." I started.

"Ambhi," he insisted. "Try it: Ambhi."

"Ambhi," I said awkwardly, as he nodded and smiled, "Has Rakti mentioned any of the others?"

"Rakti? Who is Rakti?" he asked.

"Rakti... he had me transferred here... didn't he?" I was more perplexed than ever.

"I don't know any Rakti. *I* had you transferred. I want you to teach me your wrestling holds, starting with that one from yesterday. That was the best display I saw all day. Your opponent was big and mean, and the way you stopped him... where did you learn that? You're not even of the warrior class."

He doesn't even know Rakti! I thought. Then Satu and the others don't know Rakti's story *is* a lie!

The prince looked at me, obviously not used to being kept waiting.

"Diipundi, village elder of Shaktin... he taught me and Leeta, my twin sister, the arts of The Gentle Way. He became an uncle to us after his own son was killed in the same war as my father. And he learnt it from none other than the Purple Sage."

"The Gentle Way? It didn't seem that gentle! But the Purple Sage... I have heard that name. I know, the philosophers at the University of Taxila. Anyway, it doesn't matter, let's get started."

I was proud of myself for not trying to hide where I was from. It was obvious that the prince hadn't heard of Shaktin, but at least I had been honest with him from the start.

"Your... I mean Ambhi, sorry, but I'm just finding it a bit awkward, the idea of wrestling the prince."

Ambhi laughed. "Maybe if I take my robes and turban off..." he said as he removed his turban and flung off his robes onto the floor.

"There. Is that better? Just imagine that I'm just one of your friends from, what was the name of your village again?"

"Shaktin. All right, then," I said, still finding it hard to imagine him amongst the Shaktin boys, "let's begin. I'm crouching down low in a typical readiness pose, but I'm also deliberately making my head a target to tempt you to try a headlock on me. It worked with Bazzin the other day. So, make your approach and I'll demonstrate."

The prince sprang to grasp me around the head, but, before he could tighten the hold, I instinctively swung my forearm over his shoulder and levered his head away, closing my hold and pushing his head away firmly enough to be in control but gently enough not to hurt him.

"Uuugh! Brilliant!" he cried, his arm wedged backwards in my hold. "I'm totally at your mercy!"

The thought of the prince being at my mercy made me pull back and let go immediately.

"Now show me again," he said, keen as a little boy playing with the big kids, "but slowly, so I can get it."

We went through it again but, this time, just as he went to grab my head into a headlock, I said, "Stop. Hold it there." I was surprised at my own ability to command him.

"This is what you do. Just before the opponent's arm squeezes around your head, you place your arm over his shoulder, like this, and then push hard against his head and bring your other hand on too to make it strong. When you push with full force, the opponent's arm is forced to break the headlock and the pressure on his neck and shoulder is unbearable. But then you need to push him down hard into the ground so he can't struggle and wriggle free."

"OK, now let me try."

From here, we wrestled and talked as if we had been best friends forever. It didn't take him long to learn my reverse headlock, but we practised it over and over, taking turns at being Bazzin.

We wrestled on a beautiful rug, so thick and soft, and decorated with birds and flowers.

"A gift from another kingdom," Ambhi said.

I could only imagine where the other items in this room had come from. What distant lands would they speak of if they could tell their story? A tall metallic container studded with jewels faced me. It was so elegantly shaped, with a curved handle that made you want to pick it up, and a long spout that reached from the bottom up to its full height, obviously for some rare drink that only royals have. During our wrestling bouts, objects would captivate me as Ambhi grappled with my head or my leg, and I would have to break not only his hold, but also the enchantment of his royal possessions.

After a while, we lay back exhausted. Ambhi called outside the door to a waiting servant. Before long, trays of freshly prepared food were brought in. There were so many different preparations, each in a separate bowl. Then small flatbreads were brought in hot and tender, and I could barely taste each dish before feeling full. Even then, more was brought, juicy fruits sliced open, fresh nuts toasted and spiced, and a dish that caught my eye.

Ambhi said, "Try it, Kheer, a sweet rice pudding. It's my favourite."

I stooped to pick up a bowl when there was a knock at the door. Ambhi half opened the door and stood as a voice began.

"Your Highness, Minister Treviz requests an audience. He apologises for disturbing your meal, but says it is an urgent matter of State."

"He may come back shortly," Ambhi replied. "We are not quite finished with our meal."

He shut the door and came back to our feast. "Come, eat up," he urged. "The Kheer is too good to pass up." His mood had changed. He stopped being Ambhi the village boy wrestling for fun and was once again Ambhika, Prince of Gandhara. He watched me politely while I was licking the delicious creamy rice off my fingers. I rose, realising it was time for me to leave.

"Patish, I would like you to stay a bit longer," he said. "You can wait behind that screen."

I hadn't really been listening to what they were saying, but now Ambhika's tone had caught my interest. He spoke with authority, not like a boy speaking to an elder.

"I may only be fourteen, but I am the prince!"

Squinting, I peeked through the small holes in the engraved wooden screen at the back of the prince's room.

"Forgive me, My Lord," said Minister Treviz. "I meant only to say that, because you are younger than his son, King Purushattama of Paurava is seeking to force his will upon us. It is he who sees your age as a weakness, not I, My Lordship. It is true we had hoped that a show of strength by assembling an army would be enough to avoid a war. And I agree totally My Lord that this war, like all wars, is undesirable." He paced slowly around the room as he spun his arguments. "But... it is inevitable. What we must consider foremost is our duty to the people."

I recognised the minister as one of the generals who had been with the prince on his visit to the camp when I had wrestled Bazzin. So Ambhika had to rely on ministers like Treviz to help run the kingdom, as he couldn't do it all himself.

I watched this tall figure, one hand stroking his well-oiled black beard, the other behind his back as he walked around the seated prince. Even though they were discussing such an important thing, it was the shiny redness of his embroidered gown that caught my attention. When he turned away, I saw a beautifully embroidered peacock on his back.

Again he faced the prince, his gold and silver necklaces and bracelets clinking. "I am not thinking about my own reputation or my wealth, as some would have you believe. But as your most trusted and loyal adviser, I am compelled to point out that the duty of a monarch, above all, is the welfare of the kingdom. Is it not so, Your Graciousness?"

"Honourable Treviz, the new trade routes you have opened and the new crops you have brought to the kingdom have truly brought about an increase in the wealth of all our subjects,' the prince replied. "There isn't a hut or a palace that isn't enjoying the food or the colourful cloth and ornaments that your traders have brought. Why, your name itself has come to mean prosperity in the land. But war?"

"Alas, My Lord, if the choice were so simple."

Treviz walked over to a bowl of fruit and picked up a pomegranate. Its deep crimson merged into the redness of his gown. He threw the fruit gently up into the air, catching it without taking his eyes off the prince.

"Your Lordship," he went on. "Is it not the right of your subjects to expect that their prince would improve their wealth if it were within his means? This is all that I propose. It is the King of Paurava who threatens war because he is jealous of what you have done for Gandhara!"

The prince rose and began pacing too. "What you say may be true," Ambhika said, "but it is also true that the canal we are building will affect the water supply to Paurava, especially in the dry season."

"The Pauravans themselves," Treviz responded, arms waving, "have made many canals to take the water they need, without caring how doing so affects us! In times of rain, there is plenty for all, but, in times of drought, it is our farms that suffer. The canal we are building is only to reserve for our farmers our rightful share of the water. To deny them this will result not only in reductions of crops, but loss of the precious new rice seeds we have only just begun to cultivate. The whole kingdom will suffer."

Treviz's arguments seemed to make sense, but they were to justify a war. How could a war make sense?

"For many years," the prince said, "we have been friends with Paurava. It is not an easy decision to go to war against one's friends for the sake of water."

"Yes, but true friends, Your Majesty, would not threaten war." Treviz pulled out a scroll from his robe. "This, Your Majesty, was delivered this very morning by a Pauravan courier." He unrolled it and began to read:

> Your act of diverting our water,
> is an intolerable sight.
> If by the full moon night,

this wrong is not made right,
You leave us with no option but to fight.

Treviz handed the scroll to the prince. "This is clearly the King of Paurava's seal," he added. "What choice have they given us? Is this how a friend would seek to solve a problem?"

"Nevertheless," said the prince, "let us invite King Purushattama to a meeting to discuss a mutually agreeable solution."

"A noble suggestion, My Lord, but the King of Paurava would never consider you his equal. Nor has he even hinted at any possibility for compromise. His scroll is an outright threat. He would only view a request for a meeting as a sign of weakness, and he would be further emboldened. There is only one way to respond to such a threat, and that is with force."

Treviz continued his lecture while his adornments clinked. "It is clear, the Pauravans care only for themselves and would see us suffer rather than share the water. Is it not the most preposterous proposition to ever reach Your Majesty's ears! Their water, indeed! These are not the words of a friend. As you suggest, friends discuss problems, not threaten war. The King of Paurava is trying to take advantage of your age. By threatening us with war, he believes that we will back down and destroy our new life-giving canal. That would make him look like a hero and hide his own lack of initiative. And if you give in to his threats, who knows what he would demand next?

"As you can see, there is really no choice. The people of Gandhara are completely behind you. Even villagers on the outskirts of the Kingdom feel threatened and have volunteered to join our army to fight."

Volunteered! I thought. No, we didn't! I wanted to leap out from behind the screen and shout *liar!* – but I knew better.

Minister Treviz continued. "Every prince has to prove his courage and strength before ascending to the Crown. Your father died unexpectedly before you had performed such a feat. Give your people the leader they want. They are ready to fight for you and for our kingdom's water with their blood. Fulfil your destiny as their defender and king."

The prince faced Treviz. "Once again, I heed your words of wisdom, my trusted Minister, but how can I lead our army in battle?

Until now, you said that a show of strength would be enough. That assembling an army on the river would be a deterrent and the Pauravans would back down. I agreed because I wouldn't have to fight. You know only too well that I am still not a champion warrior, and the Pauravan champions would seek me out. If I were killed, the war would be lost."

"Very true, your Majesty, but none could fault you for not leading the troops from the front. It is the Pauravan king who must lead his troops from the front as the aggressor. You have every right to command the defence of your kingdom from a control tower I shall have built at the back of the battleground. From there you will be safe, and you can command the flag signals where all can see. The glory of victory will be yours."

Ambhika paced, the silence of his footsteps a contrast to the metallic jingles of the Minister. He stopped and stood up straight, raising his chin to look up at the imposing figure who had been lecturing him.

"Well, noble Treviz, you may be right. It seems there is no choice but to go to war."

"Most wise and brave, Majesty," Treviz said. He bowed for a moment before adding, "Now, you truly act like a king." He bowed once more, turned, and left the room.

I ventured out from behind the screen.

"War it is," he said.

I frowned and tried to speak, but "Uhh…" was all I could manage as I searched for words that didn't come.

"I never like arguing with Treviz," Ambhika said, looking down as he spoke. "He manipulates me, and it's really annoying. But this time, I suppose he is right. I was thinking that my role as protector was best filled by avoiding a needless war over water. But now I can see the bigger picture. This is the hardest decision I've had to make since Father died."

It was so bewildering. Less than a moon cycle ago, I had been playing soldiers in Shaktin. Yesterday, I was a foot soldier training for a war that I didn't want to fight in or die in. Now, here I was discussing war and complexities that I didn't understand.

"My friends in the Lancers think I deserted them to get out of fighting in the war," I said finally. "We were all conscripted together from our village Shaktin, before our Manhood Ritual. Mother was so upset. She wants me to survive the war more than anything, because Father was killed in the last war, and Mother and my two sisters depend on me. We never 'volunteered'; we were dragged away from our homes and our families. Why would we want to fight in such a war?"

The look in Ambhika's eyes changed. Had I said too much? He turned his back and took a few steps, then stopped and turned around.

"I, I don't know what to say... there must have been a mistake. You heard my Chief Minister. He claims men throughout Gandhara are *volunteering* to join the army to defend our land. And it cannot be denied that Paurava is starting the war.

"What choice is there? I must show them we are strong, otherwise they'll just take over the kingdom. They're trying to take advantage of my age because I am really only a crown prince. I must prove to them, and to my kingdom, that I am capable of ruling."

He sounded as if he were trying to convince himself.

"You don't know how difficult it is to be a prince," he added. "At least you have friends. How lucky you are!"

His face was a picture of sadness. "I was going to ask you to be my personal assistant, but I will have you transferred back to your friends immediately," he said, his voice quivering, like he was holding back tears. "If that's what you want."

I was still torn between my pledge to Mother and my allegiance to Satu, but now I also felt a sense of loyalty to Ambhika too. Not because he was our ruler, but because, somehow, he trusted me with the truth as only a friend would.

"No, wait," I said. "I would be honoured to be your personal assistant."

The light in his eyes reminded me of Seera whenever I offered to give her a ride on my back.

Chapter 19: The Abode of the Purple Sage

Leeta

Our guide stopped and faced us, smiling. It was a different face to the ones that had pointed a spear not long ago. When all our words and helpless thrashing about had failed, it was Anula's joining of forefingers and thumbs to make a circle that had quietened them down. When I drew the spiral shape inside a circle in the dirt, their every expression changed. They couldn't have been kinder, taking us into their village, feeding us, and providing us with a guide.

Now, our guide stood and nodded towards a huge sandstone outcrop. She said something we couldn't understand, then took an object from within the folds of her drape. In her hands was a Wisdom Wheel, just like ours! *Was* it ours? Could they have found it? She motioned up at the treetops with her hand then held it out for us to take. Anula and I looked at each other, dumbfounded. Ours or not, I took it, smiled, and nodded with every bit of gratitude I could possibly show. She smiled at us and pressed her palms against each other in a salute. Closing her eyes and tilting her head towards us in a slight bow, she opened her eyes again with a soft smile and started to edge her way back from where we had come.

"You can't leave us here. Purple Sage, you… take… us," I motioned pointing at her, then at us, then up ahead, "to the Purple Sage." She laughed and nodded pronouncedly, motioning us forward with the palm of her hand. She kept nodding, with no sign of a doubt that she knew exactly what she was doing.

We neared the face of the rock and, as we did, I noticed what appeared to be a crack. Investigating closer I realised it was the edge of one rock, and behind it an opening wide enough to walk through. Our guide was laughing and nodding, and we thanked her in the only way we could, smiling and nodding too. She nodded once more, knowing we knew we had arrived, then turned and left.

I couldn't believe it. We were standing at the entrance to the Abode of the Purple Sage.

The opening was inviting. Earthmother had created this pathway through rock. If there was a way to save our brothers, we knew we were on the right track. I thought of Limpy, how he would have raced ahead recklessly.

"You first," said Anula. She followed me around the curved path, walls of sandstone on either side. We came to an opening and stopped, dumbfounded.

Before us was a huge expanse of gentle purple wherever we looked. Purple lavender lined rows of vegetable gardens, herbs and fruit trees. Long message flags of faded purple cloth dotted the whole abode, jutting boldly out of the ground as if to proclaim the importance of their messages. We walked down the sloping path past a cluster of plantain trees and a small rock carving. Near a group of huts, children and adults were engrossed in a game of Stones and Circles. Bees and butterflies fluttered through the air, geese and chooks and goats and cows roamed freely. All were in harmony, a village enjoying another peaceful afternoon.

"Hello!" A young voice called from nowhere. I looked around. The owner of the voice stepped forward from between clumps of lavender, a smile as big as a ripe banana across his face.

"Where is your mother?" the little boy asked. His bright, curious eyes searched for a response. Anula and I turned to each other. Where would we even start?

"Where's yours?" I asked him, bending down to his level.

"Mother is in The Cave, come," he said, grasping my hand to lead us to his mother.

"Sorry, little boy," Anula said, "we have urgent business, we can meet your mother later. Can you take us to the Purple Sage?"

He looked up at us, a blank look.

I stopped. What if this wasn't the right place? "Do you know the Pur-ple Sage?" I asked in my clearest voice.

"Mother will help," he said. "What did you bring us? Can I see?" He stepped close to my sling pack and touched it, feeling for something he might treasure. Just as I anticipated his disappointment, his eyes lit up with excitement.

"What's that?" He held on to something in the sling. I slipped it off my shoulder, untied it and pulled out the water gourd and the Wisdom Wheel.

"Do you want them?" I asked him, putting the clay wheel into his small, outstretched hand. The excitement had vanished. He held it like he would hold any common object.

"Look, Love Your Mother," he said, pointing to the message flags.

I could see rows of black prints of the Wisdom Wheel on every flag.

"It's the same!" Anula said, walking over to touch the faded purple cloth with her fingers. "This must be the right place. Thank the Earth!"

Was I hearing right? Anula thanking the Earth? I recalled Diipundi's explanation of the wheel.

"Anula, do you remember what it means? 'Wisdom is in our hearts, waiting to be found'."

"No, it's 'Love Your Mother'," the little boy interjected, "everybody knows that."

"Then take us to your mother," I said, remembering the urgency of why we were here.

He took my hand and led us towards the huts. As we approached the clearing, a monster of a man turned away from the children's game and stepped in front of us. The game stopped and everyone faced us, waiting, watching to see what would happen. Most of the children were young, younger than Seera, and standing behind them, a few adults. All wore clothing coloured in various shades of faded purple. There was something wrong with some of the men – they couldn't stand straight, bent like pomegranate branches burdened with the weight of ripening fruit.

"Hello," I said to the one confronting us, smiling and bowing my head slightly.

"That," was his response, a gruff voice contrasting a childlike innocence. My eyes instinctively searched for his as I sought to appeal peacefully to him, but he barely had a face, or at least what you would normally call a face. Behind his long overhanging hair, one eye was discernible. A bent nose butted out from above the opening that must be his mouth, and the rest of his face was like a coconut that had been crushed with a rock.

"He wants to look in the bag," said our little guide, taking my sling to show him. The man let out a small grunt as he pulled out the Wheel and held it to his nose to smell it.

"No, brother Nilumby, not for eating," said the little boy, taking the Wheel from the man's big hand the way a parent would take away a dangerous object from a child.

"We have visitors!" a woman called as she stood up from behind a bed of ready-to-pick okra, a freshly made cow dung patty in her hands. She pressed the patty amongst the others covering the wall of a hut and turned to face us. "Welcome. Praise the Spirit that guided you safely to us."

Her warm welcome immediately reminded me of Mother, but her appearance was bewildering. A purple cloth across her forehead held back a wild forest of red hair but it was her eyes, like those of Nilumby, that caught my attention. While one looked at us, the other eye confused me as it seemed to look elsewhere, somewhere to our left. Her whole presence was unnerving – the contradiction between her gentle manner and her fiery look was baffling. She dipped her hands into a container of water and washed them.

"Nilumby," she said, calmly taking control, "look, I have something here for you."

He turned to her as she took a few walnuts from a pocket in her purple drape and handed them to him. He immediately crushed one in his hand. "Girls, you look exhausted. Come, let me take care of you. My name is Liilavati. And yours?"

"I'm Anula," Anula said. "Leeta and I have come to see the Purple Sage."

"This is the Abode of the Purple Sage, isn't it?" I asked.

"Actually, it's the Abode of the Earthmother," she answered with a mischievous smile, "but the Sage does live here. What is it that you seek?"

"We're from Shaktin, we've come to ask the Sage for help... you know how... about the coming war..." I didn't know where to begin.

"Our brothers, and the prince, they're in danger..." Anula blurted out.

Before she could continue, Liilavati held up her hand. "I'd like you to have some food and rest," she said, affectionately stroking our guide's forehead and hair. "You've given our visitors a warm welcome, Vijaya, well done. Are you coming inside with us too?"

He clung to her purple garment and nodded.

We passed a garden bed of purple flowering herbs that I couldn't identify. They were covered with bees, their gentle buzzes filling the moment, the moment we had been anticipating for seven days now: meeting the Purple Sage.

"Purple Sage," she said, pointing.

Anula and I looked at each other.

She went on. "Did you know that its healing power is where the Purple Sage's name came from?"

We followed Liilavati into a large hut where a woman was busily picking stones out from drying peas. Realising we were visitors, she rose with a welcoming smile.

"Sahani, this is Leeta and Anula. Could you please arrange something for them to eat? The papaya are ripening, and will be delicious with some curd and honey from my industrious bees. Then let them rest until I send for them."

She turned to us, "Now, my sisters from Shaktin, refresh yourselves and find your Calm. You will need your Clarity to explain your story to The Sage." Then she smiled and left.

"So, you've come a long way," Sahani said. "Must be something special you're seeking. Sit down there." She disappeared through the doorway, leaving us alone with the straw mat covered in peas.

"It's all a bit weird, isn't it?" Anula said as we sat on the cool clay floor.

I was thinking there was something special about this place but not what I'd expected.

"So, what were you expecting?" I said, asking myself just as much as Anula.

"Something more like a palace, or a temple," Anula said. "The Purple Sage *is* the Sage of Sages, right?"

"I know what you mean," I said. "But a palace? Temple? No, the more I think about it, the more it makes sense. Like Liilavati said, the Abode of the Earthmother."

"So, what about those strange people then?" Anula asked. "Did you expect them too?"

"No, but I can see how they're being looked after. And I don't know if they're strange. Just different... I think."

"Maybe, but why do we have to wait?"

Anula had barely finished speaking when Sahani returned. She squatted in front of us and placed two clay pots of curd and a ripe papaya at our feet. "Ungrateful pair you are! Not unusual, though most who come here think we've nothing else to do but listen to their problems."

She left, as Anula's cheeks grew pink.

***

"I'm glad you've had some rest. Come." It was the voice of Liilavati.

We got up and followed her to a cave, its mouth partly obscured by a wide clump of densely growing bamboo, the same type that protected us from the tiger two nights ago. As we followed Mother Liilavati toward the entrance, I noticed that some of the bamboo seemed to shift sideways. I turned to see a tiger yawning and rising from rest.

"Sit, Tammy, sit!" Liilavati commanded in a low voice.

The tiger paused then obeyed, its eyes relaxing as it sank and slinked back into the bamboo shelter. My heart had risen into my throat in disbelief, and I must have looked terrified, for Mother Liilavati stepped back and gently stroked my hair and then Anula's.

"Don't be afraid," she continued. "Tammy's just being protective. I've raised him from a cub, and he wouldn't harm a fly. Well, not in the Abode anyway."

Out of my confusion, one question formed clearly in my head. The markings on the tiger's face! The three lines that met between its eyes... are tigers' markings all the same?

Long purple flags and drawings on the rock faces ornamented the entrance to The Cave. Mother Liilavati turned to us and motioned with her open hand: "Come inside."

It was like entering a place of serenity and mystery, better than any temple I could ever have imagined. In the open expanse, beams of sunlight hit long cones of sparkling rock that hung from the roof. The sweet scent of sandalwood permeated the air, and the soft splash of a tiny waterfall made the whole place feel alive.

Liilavati led us to a spot beside a burning oil lamp that illuminated a rock carving of Earthmother garlanded with dried purple flowers.

"Sit," Liilavati said, smiling. "Let me get you a drink."

We obeyed, enchanted by the whole experience. In what looked like a cooking area, she mixed our drinks.

"Please," she said, handing us each a clay cup. "May your spirit be at peace in our humble home."

I held the smooth edge of the cup to my lips. The soothing flavours of milk and honey mixed delicately with cardamon and lavender. If the gods could feed you nectar, then this was surely it.

"Now, then, tell me what brings you so far from your home."

I looked at the Earthmother covered in purple garlands, then at Anula. Liilavati smiled, sensing my confusion.

"Of course, you want to speak to the Purple Sage. Go ahead, she is listening."

Now I was really confused!

"She?" asked Anula.

"Oh, you were expecting a man!" Liilavati said. She smiled with that look that adults have when they're about to explain something to you that they know will surprise or shock you.

"Well, it's just…" I replied. "I've heard about the Purple Sage all my life and never heard about him being a woman. So, where is He, I mean, She?" I looked around. There were other people in The Cave, but none looked close enough to be listening, except for a scarred man who sat motionless nearby, staring into space.

And then it hit me. "Mother Liilavati… is it you? Are you the Purple Sage?"

"You mean we've come all this way," said Anula, "to get the help of another woman!"

I could feel my cheeks reddening.

Mother Liilavati looked at us solemnly.

"Girls, I don't know what help you are seeking or whether I can help, but first let me tell you the truth about the Purple Sage."

What could we do but nod in agreement.

"Many years ago, I was brought here as a baby by my father. My mother had died giving birth to me, and my father was unable to care for me, so he brought me here and left me to be raised by the man and woman who lived here in this isolated place far from the world of people.

They were the most gentle and loving people I've ever known, and they raised me like their own child, together with other children who were orphans or had been abandoned for some reason or another."

There was something enchanting about Liilavati that was reminding me of Mother and Diipundi. Her words painted a vivid picture as she spoke.

"Occasionally we had visitors," she continued, "people who came to be cured of an illness, or who brought someone who was impaired or possessed by mental diseases. And to every needy soul this couple gave kindness and care.

"It was said that even their words could heal, and their use of purple flowering herbs in balms and infusions became legendary for their remedial power and led to them being known as the Purple Sage.

"They were truly sages who lived among the Mountain People and learnt the greatest respect for the Earthmother and all Her creation. Their simple teaching is passed on in the Wisdom Wheel like the one you have: 'Wisdom is in our hearts, waiting to be found'."

"And…" said little Vijaya, who had been listening quietly, "Love Your Mother."

"That's so right," said Liilavati, kissing him on the forehead.

"Then that's that," Anula said. "There is no Purple Sage!"

"That's not what I meant," replied Liiavati. "Even though the original Purple Sage, or Sages to be more accurate, have passed on, whenever I venture outside my Abode, people see the purple and call *me* the Purple Sage. I neither agree nor disagree, for we all have the wisdom of the Purple Sage within us. The question is, can we silence our fears and our desires long enough to hear it? Now, tell me your story. What help are you seeking?"

When she smiled, I felt a warmth radiating from her eyes; when she spoke, her words were soothing like a magical balm empowered by Truth. She was everything I had imagined the Purple Sage to be.

"The war… have you heard about the war?" I asked.

"The last war I know of," said Mother Liilavati, "was ten years ago, when we saved brothers Nilumby, Lamara, and the silent Namki from among the discarded on the battlefield. Poor souls, they had been left for dead after the injured had been taken, and their injuries were so horrific that it was nothing short of a miracle that they survived, even if they are not quite who they used to be. But you must be talking of a new war, for many moon cycles have passed since we last had visitors from your land."

I nodded. "Well, my twin brother Patish has been conscripted by the prince, and he is the only man left in our family, for my father was killed in the last war. And Patish isn't of age – he hasn't even had his Manhood Ceremony." I could see Mother Liilavati understood. "It is a wrong that must be righted," I added.

"My brother Rakti has been conscripted too," Anula said, "but Mother got him into the palace guards so he wouldn't have to actually fight." Glancing at me, she continued. "Mother worked at the palace a few years ago before we moved back to Shaktin. That's how she arranged it for Rakti.

"And that's not all. On our way here, we overheard a band of assassins who were plotting the murder of the prince and his guards. They have archers who will come from behind during the battle and shower the prince with a barrage of arrows."

The Purple Sage held up the Wisdom Wheel. "I see. And who gave you this? Was it the sage Diipundi who sent you from Shaktin? It is a long time since I last saw him."

Liilavati's eyes lit up as she mentioned Diipundi. He must have known that SHE was the Purple Sage! I felt my excitement and hopefulness rising.

"But what can we do?" Anula cried. "We are only girls – no one will listen to us!"

Her words stung me. "What do you mean? There must be something we can do." I looked to Mother Liilavati for confirmation.

"When was the last time you changed the mind of a man, then?" Anula demanded of me.

I turned to Mother Liilavati. "It was on our last day back in Shaktin when Seera, my little sister, and I stepped in front of an injured monkey to stop the boys from throwing stones at it. We saved its life."

Anula laughed. "So, you would have us go and stand between the armies and say: 'now go home and stop fighting'?"

"Exactly!" I said. "Why couldn't we?"

"Your idea has some merit," Mother Liilavati said, "but… would they listen to two young women?" She spoke as if she were asking herself the question.

"But if you came with us, they'd listen to *you!*"

Liilavati glanced around the cave. "Maybe. Maybe not. But who would look after our Family here? Look at them, they couldn't survive on their own. Some of them have conditions that only I can manage."

Her words hung in the air.

"Yes," I said. "They depend on you, Mother Liilavati. Though it's unfair to ask you. But I can't give up. It's not only Patish; the prince's life is at stake, too. I must go, even if I have to go alone."

I avoided Anula's eyes – I couldn't believe she would give up after all we'd been through. I couldn't rely on her anymore.

No one spoke, until the silence was broken by a voice nearby. "AAA… AAALL… ALL… all go."

It was the man who had been sitting staring into space. The light fell on his face, a face that spoke of pain and misery, with only one eye, yet there was goodness in that eye.

"Namki!" said Mother Liilavati, surprised. "He has never spoken before." She walked over to him. "For ten years, we've waited for you to find your voice! Oh Namki!" She put her hand gently on his hair and lifted it back off his face, continuing to stroke his head slowly, like she would a baby. "You have chosen this moment to speak. What is it you are saying? Try it again slowly."

"Wwwe – muuust – AAaLLll…ALL GGOo," he said, almost choking to get the words out.

"All go? ALL GO! You want everyone to go with me, is that it? Well, yes, why not, let us *all* go!"

I frowned. "But it will take too long… I mean, if everyone is coming. The Mountain is steep, and the animals… we got into trouble more than once. Would it be safe for children?" Thinking of Limpy, I added, "or safe for Namki?"

Liilavati gazed deep into the cave. Then she smiled. "You are right, dear Leeta, but I know a safer way. Now, we have no time to lose. Let us make our plan."

Chapter 20: Patish's Battle Eve

The drinking and feasting had stopped. The chanting had stopped. The drumming had stopped. The tales of heroics from past wars had stopped. The speeches about loyalty and sacrificing our lives for prince and country had stopped. The blessing rituals and the reminders of the holiness of honour and duty had stopped.

An unnerving quiet set in. One night remained before the battle.

In the silence, a dread of death gripped me. Out of nowhere it came, spreading like a wildfire inside me while I slept. I was covered in sweat and could hardly breathe. For a few long moments I froze, my thoughts a jumbled mess of fear and panic.

Suddenly, I had to empty my bowels. I got up from my sleeping mat and headed for the nearest latrine, squeezing my buttocks, desperate. When I reached it, I couldn't believe the queue of soldiers ahead of me. The pressure was so bad I could barely contain it.

"Sorry, I'm desperate, could I go next, brother?" I pleaded to the soldier at the front of the line. His reluctant grunt was the sweetest grace to my ears, and I thanked him repeatedly as I entered after another soldier vacated the pit. I squatted just in time and the expulsion that followed was instant relief. As my stomach muscles relaxed and my breathing calmed, I became aware of the sounds and smells around me – I wasn't the only one with the runs. To know you will engage with death shortly, and that your own fate is out of your hands, is enough to scare the shit out of anyone.

I was too restless to go back to sleep, too agitated to even try. Since we had arrived at the battlefield that evening, one thought kept troubling me: I would be in relative safety amongst the palace guards at the back of the battlefield while Satu and our brothers from Shaktin would be in the most dangerous position in the front line. Yet this was the very thing I had promised to Mother and Leeta and Seera – to do anything to survive.

As we set up the Royal camp, I saw a platform had been built behind the edge of the riverbank, elevated with a view across the sands of the riverbed where the various units of the Gandharan army were assembling. There was no sign yet of the lancers who I knew would be at the front, but that didn't stop me from looking for anyone from Shaktin.

My attention had strayed to the vast army of Paurava, which spread as widely as ours. All that separated us was a shallow rivulet, easy to run through when the battle began. With monsoonal rains, the mighty Jhelum River would become a torrent and make a battle impossible. But with a clear sky above, there was little hope of that happening.

What could I say to Prince Ambhika? Whatever I said would be so out of place, compared to the guards who would doubtlesssly remain silent. The prince's every word, his every command, were treated with a blind acceptance. I couldn't get used to it. We had become such good friends in these last few days, and it was his trust in me that was making me uneasy now.

My hands felt cold and my muscles were flexing, shivering, so I clasped the refuge around my neck, Father's sun, and fixed my mind on my breathing: in slowly and out slowly, imagining everything around me dissolving away. Oh, for the blissful fields of Shaktin!

***

"Patish, wake up. How can you sleep at such a time? I want you to be with me."

I opened my eyes to see Prince Ambhika standing above me. Guards behind him held flaming torches, but I could see it was first light, the beginning of pre-dawn. I rose to my feet and followed him to the platform, where advisors and generals were arriving for their final orders.

"Your Majesty," I said. Then, knowing we were in the earshot of others, I lowered my voice and asked, "Could we talk?"

I knew that this was hardly the time, with him engrossed in the preparations, but he bent down to listen.

"Ambhika," I started, suddenly unsure of myself. "I want to ask for a favour."

"Speak," he said without hesitation. "But I think I know what you are going to ask."

"I want to say that I am so grateful for your friendship and trust and do so wish that our friendship will continue... but... to be true to myself, I must ask to join my brothers from Shaktin," I said.

"On the front line, right?" he said. "Well, they are lucky to have such a friend as you. And I am honoured that you call me your friend also." He pondered for a moment then went on. "Because I value your friendship, I must come, too!"

Before I could say anything, he called to his Chief Minister.

The minister paused his conversation with the commanders and walked over to us. "Patish and I are going to join the lancers in the front line. Please make whatever arrangements are necessary."

Never before had I seen a face change so completely in such a short time.

The minister's face contorted with a reddening rage that he barely restrained to address the prince. "Your Majesty, this is impossible! How can your safety be guaranteed? Even your Royal Guards and Champions of Gandhara will not be able to protect you! They are all ready, in their positions with the strategies our commanders have prepared. Such a change would cause chaos! Your duty must direct the battle with the commanders from the safety of the platform. It would demoralise the whole army if they learned of such a reckless change, and they would question your sanity! I beg you, Sire, put the good of the kingdom first, and desist from this plan."

Overhearing, Commander Vinyak stepped forward. "What Minister Treviz says is true, Your Majesty, it is too late to change the plans. It would only cause confusion and unfairly disadvantage our men. The enemy is ready to attack at any moment."

The king paused, then turned to me. "I suppose it is so. I must do my duty just as you must do yours. But whatever happens, our friendship must remain, Patish, will you promise me that?"

"I will honour your friendship as I honour the rising of my Father's sun, Your Majesty."

Chapter 21: Leeta's Battle Eve

We reached a wide, sandy clearing stretching out beyond the trees. It was a still night, but I was sure it must be the river Jhelum. A cluster of rocks presented an opportunity for a better view.

"Mother, stop everything, while I climb the rocks to see if the army camps are within sight."

Mother held up her crossed arms to pass on the 'Stop' signal we had been using. Soon, hundreds of women behind us sat quietly down to wait. That's what we were now – a women's peace army.

I was still coming to terms with how readily the women of the valley had joined us as we'd gone from one village to the next. Mother knew many of them from the valley Harvest Festival we went to every year. When she spoke about losing Father and now Patish being taken, they knew the pain too. Like us, they'd had enough. And when I had said the Sage would lead us…

As I started to climb, I heard footsteps behind me. "Me, too, I want to see the Sage." It was Seera.

The moon was full and lit the sky, but occasional clouds drifted across to dim its brightness. I wondered if that was some kind of a sign from Earthmother. Maybe She would pelt the land with a downpour to stop the war before it could even start. But my hopes faded in the darkness; I could see these clouds were just drifters, the kind that teased us long before torrential rains would fall.

Downstream, a glow was visible on either side of the river: bonfires, and with them, pulsating chants accompanied by the thumping of drums. We could almost see the armies of Gandhara and Paurava gathered on either side of the tranquil length of water that separated them, around great sacrificial fires, invoking the grace of the gods of fire and destruction as they worked themselves into a frenzy for tomorrow's battle.

Somewhere amongst them was Patish, helpless and waiting, waiting for the dawn and for the battle to follow. Like every soldier on both sides of the river, he was about to confront the unknown. What fate lay hidden behind the sunrise... life or death? I longed to tell him not to worry, that we were here, so close, and that our plan to stop the war was in the hands of none other than the Purple Sage. I closed my eyes to send him my love and my hope, heart to heart.

I opened my eyes to see Seera, waiting.

"We must be close to our meeting point," I said, thinking of the darkness between us and the distant bonfires.

"What if the Sage has not come?" Seera said. "What if they got lost?"

I hadn't considered that. "She'll be here," I replied, knowing that the alternative was unthinkable. "Let's climb down; we have no time to lose."

Our army walked in the light of the full moon, the soft sand of the riverbed squeaking beneath our feet. We approached a massive boulder that obscured our vision upstream. It had to be the outcrop where we would meet, just like Liilavati had said. We halted and the women sat to rest, whispers of expectation passing among them. I went ahead, around the rock. I had taken but a few steps when I heard a voice.

"Leeta." It was She, Liilavati, the Purple Sage. Behind her, I could see the shadowy shapes of her Family in slumber on the sand. "Thanks to the help of the Mountain People, we have arrived in time! And it seems you have brought your whole valley with you!"

Murmurs of excitement spread amongst the women who poured past the rock and crowded round to see the One who embodied the hope they clung to. A growl from the deep throat of a tiger startled the crowd.

"Tammy, hush, we are with friends," Liilavati reassured him.

The shadowy Tammy lay down.

"Welcome to you all, courageous people of the valley," Liilavati said. "Take your rest now, for we have some time before we move."

"Please meet Mother and my sister Seera," I said to her, gesturing toward Mother and Seera.

They clasped their palms in a greeting of respect to the Sage.

"I am so honoured to meet you both," the Sage replied. "Let us sit and talk."

We sat in a small circle with her.

"Leeta, are you ready?" she asked.

In the moonlight, I could see her beaming eyes prying into my heart.

"Yes," I answered, "as ready as I can be."

Her eyebrows moved ever so slightly, her gaze intensifying as if to see me more clearly.

"But my head is so full of thoughts," I added, knowing I was stating the obvious.

"Tell me," she said.

I paused. "I... I guess I *am* afraid... a little. Not really for myself – strangely I'm not afraid of what we have to do, more afraid of what will happen if we fail." I felt my cheeks reddening in the darkness as I realised that my words revealed my lack of faith. "I feel like I've convinced everyone to be here, that we've trusted each other, but I'm not sure about..." I didn't know how else to say it. I had to be honest. "Anula."

"Where *is* Anula?" Liilavati asked.

"She's meant to be meeting us here, too. With her mother and women from Paurava." Saying it out aloud made me conscious of my doubt.

"When we reached Shaktin and told our mothers everything that had happened," I went on, "Anula's mother, Hileena, looked down with shame. But then she told us this: 'It is true that I sent Anula to slow down Leeta, but I didn't think she had any real chance of getting the Purple Sage's help. I expected the plan would fail anyway, so why not at least take advantage of it? I know it was completely selfish, but in my fear of the war, I saw it as an opportunity to save my son Rakti by getting him into the Palace Guards. Now you tell me that assassins will attack the prince and his guards from behind, putting Rakti in even greater danger! Surely, it is the gods punishing my selfishness! I have learned my lesson. I do not only beg your forgiveness, I will also embrace your plan, Leeta.'"

"But..." interceded Liilavati, "you said she was to meet us here with women from Paurava. How will she do that?"

"That's what really surprised me," I said. "I mean, we were all amazed with what she said next: 'While you and your mother go to the Valley villages to gather their women, Anula and I will enlist the help of Sotiira, my late husband's cousin who married a trader from the Pauravan side of the Jhelum River. She doesn't want the war either and will surely help. Like us, Pauravan women will join in once they hear the Purple Sage is intervening."'

I paused again, "That's what she *said*, but what if Hileena and Anula have betrayed us again? We could be walking into a trap."

Mother's lips opened, but Liilavati spoke before she could say anything.

"What you say could be true," Liilavati said gently. "I know you were betrayed once by Anula, and it is not easy to trust someone after that has happened. But I trust her, for, at the Abode when we made our plan, I felt the truth behind her words. There could be many explanations for why she is not here, and yet she may arrive soon for all we know. All is not lost."

Her voice was a calming balm, and I continued to listen.

"It is difficult to know what the right thing to do is at times like this, but what choices do we have? Either we go on, or turn back. If we turn back, we will have failed in our mission, and, if Anula and her mother succeed in bringing the women of the Pauravan villages from across the river, we will have failed them also."

I wanted to believe and to trust, like a child being guided by an adult. But the doubts persisted like a pesky fly, and I shook my head in shameful defiance. "Even if they turn up, what if we still fail...? What if the battle begins? There will be no stopping it." I couldn't hold back my tears, not even when I closed my eyes. "I so badly want to save Patish," I went on, "but now Mother and Seera are in danger. And I've brought you and your Family into it, too."

"No, Leeta," said Liilavati. "I made my own decision, and you heard Namki. What he said was what we all felt – *all* go. We are all in this together."

Liilavati's hand caressed my forehead. "Leeta, you are right to feel afraid and to ask these questions. There is no shame in fear. But we must now trust in our own judgement and do what we believe is right. Some things are out of our hands, and we have no control over them. We only can control the things we do, and we have chosen to do this to stop this war, haven't we?"

I knew she was right. I knew it in my body and in my soul. "Yes," I answered, "that's what we are here for. To stop the war."

Chapter 22: Time for War

Patish

A slow drumbeat began, the signal that the whole army was assembled and waiting. Squadron flags were upright, ready to be raised. Satu stood on my right, and to his right was Tomay. We were in the frontline of Lancers. We didn't speak, but the tight-lipped smiles of recognition we exchanged were enough for me to know I was with brothers.

The dark morning sky began turning blue. I could hear the distant Pauravan army, but they were hidden by a mist over the river. Was it Nature's way of keeping us apart until the very last moment? Then the inevitable: the mist brightened with light.

I could make out spearheads high above the heads of the Pauravan lancers, catching the first rays from the sun. They glittered across the riverbed like ominous charms.

The bronze tip of Satu's tightly held lance had become almost a part of him as he wielded it, jabbed, parried and blocked during training, joust after joust. But now I knew that these were no longer the toys of boys playing, they were weapons to kill. A Pauravan soldier would soon be charging at Satu, driven by the instinct to survive and the will to return to his own loved ones. He would have to drive the lance deep into Satu's flesh before Satu did it to him.

With my lance, I would be a Pauravan target, too, and I would have to kill if I did not want to be killed.

Would the Pauravans charge first? I wondered.

As our armies waited for the signals of our leaders, a shadow emerged from the sky. I expected a cloud, but it was a huge flock of white swans flying overhead, with an eerie flapping of wings.

"Omen!" a soldier said, his whisper echoing down the line.

"Look, what's that in the mist?" cried a voice.

I gripped my lance harder.

As the mist lifted, I could see figures moving slowly along the river, but not towards us. Clearly not Pauravan soldiers, they looked like bedraggled beggars seeking a place to rest. I made out children and women, and a few old men, bent and walking with limps. There were about twenty or thirty, all wearing rags of varied shades of purple. And a tiger with them!

"The Purple Sage!" exclaimed someone before a chorus broke out. "Purple Sage… Purple Sage… Purple Sage…."

To add to the spectacle, the swans that had been circling high above now started landing on the water as if it were just another calm day.

Both armies paused to watch in wonder. A moment ago, we were poised for battle. Now, bewilderment dominated.

A soldier behind me pronounced, "The Wise One". His eyes were wide open as if witnessing a miracle.

"The Compassionate One," cried a guard near Commander Rixten, who just looked on.

"The Enlightened One," came a voice from a flag bearer. Talking broke out through the ranks, all of it about the Purple Sage.

The drum doubled its beat trying to regain control. It was the final signal of readiness, but then it stopped. The Lancers' flag leant forward, our signal to lower lances to the horizontal to engage with the enemy. But the Pauravans were not attacking. Were we being ordered to charge the Purple Sage?

Then another surprise! Women streamed in from the same direction that the Sage had come from. Hundreds of them moved alongside the Sage, as the swans flapped their wings, shifting to accommodate the new arrivals.

I tried to spot the prince on his command platform but my vision stopped at Minister Treviz, who I recognised among a group of generals on horseback. The look on his face! He'd been preparing for his moment of glory, and now everything was falling into disarray.

Fuming, he motioned to his dog keeper, then shouted, "Attack! Kill!"

Four long-haired slender hounds, Afghans, raced off, growling and barking towards the purple clothed ones. I watched in horror. Soldiers clenched their lances. No orders came from the squadron commanders.

But then the dogs skidded to a halt a few steps away from the ragged group, their snarls changing to yelps as a swarm of bees threatened them before a deep growl from the tiger dropped them to the ground like frightened puppies.

The Purple Sage stepped forward to pat the dogs that rolled over like pets playing with their master.

With two armies mesmerised at the sight, the Sage stood up tall and took off a purple shawl, holding it up high before tearing it in two. Two women stepped forward to receive one piece each. They held the purple cloth up high above their heads like flags of peace, then one of them started heading for the Pauravan side while the other headed almost straight towards us.

I couldn't believe my eyes – it was Leeta!

As she crossed the dry sandy riverbed onto the bank where our army was assembled, she couldn't see me amongst the thousands of soldiers.

"Let me through, I have a message for the prince," she hollered.

"Kill her!" Treviz commanded his royal guards. "She could be an assassin."

Four guards drew their swords and moved towards Leeta while other soldiers moved back, opening the space.

"Don't touch her – she's my sister!" I yelled, lowering my lance to defend her. Two lances pointed at the guards. Holding the other was Satu.

"Kill them, too!" shouted Treviz, "And begin the attack! Trumpeters, sound the war cry. Flagmen, signal advance!"

The guards turned to Satu and me as we shielded Leeta, but stopped, seemingly confused by what was happening around us. Other soldiers stepped forward to join us. I could see Martal, Tomay, Sujas, Asten, Liddu, Janam, Laksa, Talbik and even the Rolpur boys Vinto and Solti. And, to my total surprise, Bazzin and Slicer, too!

"Kill them ALL!" Treviz bellowed.

As a group of royal guards moved forward to attack, one of them ran out in front and yelled, "No, this is a mistake; they're from Shaktin."

It was Rakti, but before he could continue, a guard knocked him to the ground. Then, swords drawn, they marched toward us.

"STOP!" came a booming cry of authority. Instant silence followed, except for the rearing and snorts of two horses halting.

Riding on one was Commander Vinyak, and, on the other, the prince.

"Stop!" repeated the prince, dismounting. "Let her speak."

To add further confusion, from behind the army came the thudding sounds of arrows pelting into wood, and a few screams.

"Archers, from behind!" cried a voice from near the royal platform in the rear. "They're on horseback, fleeing!"

Leeta walked forward, catching her breath as she looked up at the prince.

"Your Majesty, my name is Leeta, and this is my brother Patish. I came to warn you about the archers. My friend and I overheard them plotting. They planned to assassinate you when the battle started, but, luckily, as we can all see, your wisdom has foiled their plan."

The prince stood, speechless. His decision to leave the Royal platform to save me had saved him from the barrage of assassins' arrows.

"I also have a request from the Purple Sage," Leeta continued. "She wishes to speak to you."

"What insolence!" Treviz fumed as he reached the scene. "That fool, how dare *he* command the prince. Your majesty, we cannot tolerate such indignity."

"I'm sorry, Your Royal, Sir, um Lord ..." Leeta said, blushing. "This is not a command, only a request, an invitation. And the Purple Sage is not a 'he', she is a woman."

"Woman?" he queried. The word 'woman' spread throughout the soldiers.

"Women!" said the soldier next to the king and Treviz, pointing towards the river.

"I know!" snapped Treviz, staring at the Purple Sage and the rag-covered troupe that surrounded her.

The unreality of the situation was growing. Along both sides of the riverbed, even more women streamed in. They were young and old, some with children clutching their mothers' hands. After the Purple Sage motioned to them, the women locked arms and sat facing the armies on both sides.

The young Prince of Gandhara summoned his guard. "My horse."
Treviz ordered, "And mine."

"No!" commanded Prince Ambhika. Treviz bowed his head in reluctant acceptance.

"Leeta," said the prince, stepping towards her, "your courage saved my life. I am forever grateful. Now, take me to your sage. And Patish..." he said to me, "won't you come, too?" He didn't need my answer before commanding two more horses be brought to him.

We waited for the prince to mount his white steed with platted mane and tail before mounting our own horses and following him down the riverbank. The women parted to let us through, bowing their heads as the prince passed. We reached the Purple Sage and dismounted after the prince.

The Pauravan king arrived on a huge, colourfully attired war elephant. It turned side on and knelt gracefully for the monarch to get down. He took a few steps towards the Sage and stood next to the prince.

"My Respected Lords," the Purple Sage said, her crisp voice piercing the silence while she motioned gently, opening her hands towards both sides of the river, "your kingdoms have been neighbours and friends for as long as my memory goes back.

"You, King Purushattama, are known and respected throughout your land and beyond as a great man of courage, compassion and wisdom.

"You, Prince Ambhika, have been ruling your kingdom since the unfortunate and untimely death of your father. Your realm houses the University of Taxila, unmatched for the wisdom it has accumulated from every civilisation in the world. But of what worth is such knowledge unless it can serve us all today? You are a monarch with wisdom beyond your age, and it is with this wisdom that you can solve the problem being faced by your people."

Any doubt I'd ever had about the Purple Sage had been demolished. She stood over a prince and a king with the authority like that of Mother over me. And she wasn't finished yet. "In times of drought, the lack of water is indeed a problem. But is war the answer?" She looked around beyond the royals, casting her gaze across to each army in turn. This was a question for us all.

"It is not the first-time kingdoms have gone to war over precious water, but does that make it right? A century ago, two kingdoms to the east threatened war until the Great Enlightened Prince of Peace asked them to think of righteousness and consider which is of greater value: blood or water?"

She held out her hands toward them. "Look upon your armies. What do you see? Soldiers? Yes, but look again.

"These men are husbands and sons, fathers and grandfathers, brothers, and uncles, and they are not alone. Their wives and daughters, mothers and grandmothers, sisters and aunts have left their saddened homes and villages to be with their men, for if their men are killed today, their lives are lost, too."

Then she turned toward her purple clad ones. "See my own Family assembled before you. They are the products of war. Children orphaned and abandoned; soldiers left for dead on the battlefield, maimed beyond recognition. They chose to leave the safety of their mountain refuge to show you how war destroyed their lives, for life is the most precious and sacred gift of all. So, I ask you, great kings, show us the compassion and wisdom you have been blessed with. Please consider: Which is of greater value – blood or water?"

Prince Ambhika replied immediately. "Blood, of course."

"Blood," agreed the King of Paurava.

"Then why spill the blood of your faithful subjects instead of sharing this precious water in peace?"

Prince Ambhika bowed his head.

"THIS WAR…" he declared, gazing across to the soldiers awaiting his command, "IS NO MORE! Fill in the new canal. We will not deprive our friends, the Pauravans, of their share of water."

Chapter 23: Epilogue – One More Question

Leeta

A ll Taxila seemed to be one big party. There were men of all ages, many still wearing the red of the Gandharan army uniform; women in brightly coloured wraps usually kept for weddings and festivals; and in the middle of the marketplace, a band of drummers, trumpeters and minstrels leading chanting crowds who surrounded them. Children dancing and laughing made a line like a snake and started winding through the swarm of people. Street vendors' cries let us know that their curds were the freshest, their spice patties the hottest, and their sweets so tasty they would delight even the Elephant God and his devoted servant mouse. But what stood out the most were the looks on their faces: sparkling eyes and broad smiles that kept bursting into laughter.

The war was over.

Not a single wife or child had to grieve. The dark threat that had engulfed every person in the land was now gone – like a storm that menaced but vanished with the wind.

Everything was so unrealistic, I felt like I was alive in some wonderful mythological story as it was being created.

We walked behind the Purple Sage and her Family and, as people realised who She was, they stopped and stared, or prostrated and touched Her feet, or sprinkled Her with jasmine flowers and rose petals. In front of me was young purple-clad Vijaya holding the hand of the war-damaged survivor Nilumby. After years of isolation at the Purple Sage's Abode, he and the other survivors were celebrating their return from the horrors of injury caused by war.

I couldn't have been more enchanted if Earthmother herself parted the skies and showered us with shooting stars, or the clouds above formed into an open lotus flower and sprinkled us with lotus seeds to show Her divine approval.

Holding Mother with my left hand, and Seera with my right, and with Patish walking behind us with Satu, I was in bliss. My whole body was bursting with delight. I shot a smile to Anula who walked with her mother beside us, but before she could respond, a noisy disturbance broke out ahead. The crowd parted as we approached.

A richly robed man with a long black beard and jewelled turban was shouting in anger. He glared towards us, waving his hands in gestures of rage. I stopped. Mother and Seera did the same. But the Sage and her Family continued. Mother glanced at me, and we began walking again to keep up with the Sage.

"Detestable woman of loathsome falsehood!" he cried. A hush settled over the onlooking crowd.

"Vile spreader of unspeakable lies!" he screamed as his eyebrows met in fury.

I was perplexed – his abuse was directed at the Sage! I picked up our pace, pulling on Mother's and Seera's hands. Once again, I was overwhelmed with a protective urge, this time for the Sage and the innocent ones who so dearly depended on her for life and soul.

"Swindler of Gandhara's indomitable rights for water!
Heartless robber of wealth for the people!
Contemptible supporter of inferior Gods!
Despicable spoiler of divinely made plans!
Atrocious deceiver of young Royals!"

The daylight dimmed from the darkness of his words. Never had I ever heard such language. His eyes bulged and were ready to burst. He pointed his finger then clenched his fist, but he kept on without a pause.

"Obnoxious leader of wild animals!
Beastly keeper of stinging insects!
Uncultivated recluse of the jungle!
Unsavoury purveyor of deception!"

The raging madman edged forward, yet the Purple Sage, unchanging in her manner, continued at her gentle pace, her Family behind her.

"Repulsive representative of all that is a sham!
Insufferable instigator of injustice!
Nauseating nuisance!
Execrable eater of undergrowth!
Ghastly gatherer of the discarded!"

He stopped right in front of Her, arms waving wildly, eyes about to pop, veins protruding from his neck. She stood calmly waiting for him to finish, but still he found more to say.

"Obnoxious, sickening, nasty, repugnant, atrocious, abominable, appalling, abysmal, frightful…"

Then he stopped, probably running out of words or breath. The Sage tilted her head up ever so slightly and spoke, her sweet, firm voice a welcome change to the coarseness of his ranting and raving.

"O Minister Treviz, we meet again. Once more we hold divergent views, but I offer you my greetings. Now, I have a philosophical question for you. If you offer me a pomegranate, but I decline to accept it, will the pomegranate not remain with you?"

The minister stared intently, bewildered. He was unable or unwilling to answer.

The Sage spoke again. "Then, similarly, I decline to accept your words."

A drop of rain hit my nose. Earthmother had held off long enough. Pouring rain started to fall from the heavens as Mother, Patish, Seera and I moved forward to hug and farewell Mother Liilavati and her Family. Little Vijaya stood out in front, the tears in his eyes merging with the raindrops that were now drenching us. I picked him up in an embrace to give him the biggest hug ever.

Mother was facing Namki when he brushed aside the long hair that always covered his face, or what remained of it. Wounds to his left eye, nose and part of his mouth had somehow merged, with common folds of skin that resembled the molten wax of a candle. I saw Mother's jaw drop.

"I pity the poor woman you belong to, you poor, poor soul!" she said, her eyes glazing over in a stare of shock.

Namki straightened himself to stand as tall as Mother. He lifted his deformed chin, wiped the raindrops from his face and looked at her with his one good eye.

"D D... De... DDev...ki!" he stuttered, spreading out his arms.

Mother gasped, her hands pressing her cheeks like she'd seen a ghost. "Rewoldji?"

Patish and I looked at each other.

"Father?"

Historical Notes on *Earthrunner*

Taxila and the non-violent culture of the village Shaktin in *Earthrunner*

Ancient Taxila was a wealthy city of Gandhara situated between the Indus and Jhelum rivers, a pivotal junction for the overland trade between the Indian subcontinent and several parts of Western Asia and Central Asia. Once known as the seat of oriental cultures and learning, it had the ancient world's first international university.

Perhaps its greatest virtue, however, was a culture rich in the ideas of non-violence that have pervaded India right through the ages. While the history of India abounds in chapters of war and conflict, the Gandharan civilization of Taxila was a point of confluence for a number of powerful non-violent ideologies.

The first of these was the peaceful culture left behind by the ancient Indus Valley Civilization where 2000 cities had flourished for 700 years until 1700 BCE. In *The Story of India*, historian Michael Wood wrote: "Strangest of all for the archeologists is that they found no evidence of war and conflict." In thousands of Indus Valley artifacts, there are none depicting warfare or killing.

Around 500 BCE, Mahavira, often called the founder of Jainism, and Siddhartha Gautama, known as the Buddha, presented radical non-violent reforms for their time. Each promoted a life of peace and meditation over conflict and the horrors of war. The village of Shaktin in *Earthrunner*, home of Patish and Leeta, portrays a 'Way of Peace', a fictional culture influenced by non-violent teachings such as these and others.

Our creation of the Purple Sage, a mythical woman of peace who calms vicious hounds and warring kings, is our way of recognizing the peace-making role of women that is so common yet so often ignored by history. The colour purple was chosen for its broad association with peace and justice, and its history within the Women's Liberation Movement.

It is also important to note that we have chosen to present *Earthrunner* in westernized voices to facilitate its accessibility, especially for younger readers. While the story has a specific context in a specific time and place, we have simplified it to represent a more universal story. No disrespect is meant to the great cultures and religions of India.

Conscription and War – Another Perspective

While historians focus on powerful kings and the strategies of generals, our focus is on how common people are affected by war.

The perspective of Patish on being conscripted was developed from Constantine's experience. When I was aged twenty, and the voting age was twenty-one, the Australian government was using conscripted soldiers to support its war efforts in the Vietnam War, as was its ally, the U.S.A.

I chose non-violent action as a draft resistor, was arrested for exercising my right to free speech and handing out leaflets inciting young men not to register for conscription, and actively joined the hundreds of thousands of musicians, journalists, writers, philosophers, religious heads, politicians, union leaders, students, teachers, mums, dads and returned soldiers who all combined to form the unstoppable anti-war movement that brought an end to the Vietnam War.

In *Earthrunner*, Patish is conscripted in unjust circumstances, taken before his Manhood Ceremony and after his own father had been killed in a previous war. An unnecessary war over water, it was more about increasing production and wealth, not survival. Sadly, even in modern times, examples abound of boys and girls as young as twelve being stolen to fight.

The Way of Peace in *Earthrunner* is not an absolute dictum of pacifism, rather it is a pragmatic principle: live in a way that causes the least harm possible to others. Self-defence or defence of the innocent is therefore not only acceptable but also desirable. The village elder Diipundi is a mentor to both Patish and Leeta, training them in yoga, mindfulness, martial arts and Earthrunning.

Leeta refuses the role of a helpless onlooker and shows the courage and initiative of a peacemaker willing herself to make a difference.

The arrival of women in the novel from both sides to force a ceasefire for negotiating peace is based on the non-violent actions of women in many real situations around the world. It is not intended to simplistically generalise peacemaking along gender lines, but it may be worth considering the special peacemaking contributions of women. In real life, Lehmah Gbowee inspired Christian and Muslim women to refuse to sleep with their husbands until they ended the bloody 14-year civil war in Liberia. She, together with two other women, Tawakkol Karman of Yemen and Ellen Johnson Sirleaf also of Liberia, were awarded the 2011 Nobel Peace Prize.

Who can argue with the rights of mothers to defend their sons? In 1965, Save Our Sons was established in Sydney to oppose conscription and the Vietnam War. Under its banner groups formed all over Australia and around it the Anti-Vietnam War and Anti-Conscription movements grew.

And then there is Malala Yousafzai. When she was a fifteen-year-old speaking up for the rights of girls in Pakistan to learn, an extremist shot her in the head. She survived the near fatal wound and established the Malala Fund, a charity championing the rights of girls around the world to an education. In 2014 she received the Nobel Peace Prize, the youngest-ever Nobel laureate. It is purely coincidental that Malala was born in the Swat Valley, close to the setting of *Earthrunner*.

There is of course much more that could be said about the great advocates of peace throughout the ages. But the story of *Earthrunner* is not an essay on the history of non-violence, rather it is a fictional story attempting to portray some of the realities of the common people living in a place preparing for war. The focus of the writing has always been on the feelings and thoughts of the protagonists Leeta and Patish in every situation they faced. Our writing about non-violence is not ideological, but based on the simple belief that most people, privileged with agency, will choose the way of peace.

– Simone and Constantine Pakavakis